2/14   NK

30127 08261882 3

Suffolk County Council	
30127 08261882 3	
Askews & Holts	Oct-2014
AF	£13.30

All rights of distribution, also by film, radio, television, photomechanical reproduction, sound carrier, electronic media and reprint in extracts, are reserved.

The author is responsible for the content and correction.

© 2013 united p. c. publisher

Printed in the European Union, using environmentally-friendly, chlorine-free and acid-free paper.

www.united-pc.eu

Hilton James.
TALES FROM SLEEPY DOG LAND 2.
RAGNAR'S TOOTH.

TALES FROM SLEEPY DOG LAND 2.
INTRODUCTION.

When our dogs take a nap so their spirits take flight
straight to Sleepy Dog Land
anytime - day or night.
Safe in Sleepy Dog Land
where all dogs may roam free
or hangout with their mates
"neath The Happiness Tree.
Tasty treats there aplenty
lushous grass just to chew
anything they could want for
every wish will come true.
Such a magical haven
where no dog has a care
It's a realm of true wonder
In amidst of a prayer.

Sleepy Dog Land is to be found on the edge of a dream.
It is a truly wonderful place.
A place filled full with magic and happiness.
The doggy variety of course.
Sleepy dog land is well known and used on a regular
basis by dogs.
Dogs of every size shape and breed. House dogs, wild
dogs, working dogs and prize winning dogs.
Every caniane of every type that you could possibly
think of are there or have been - or will at some point,
be found chilling out - under Sleepy Dog lands deepest
of blue skys.
Now, are you wondering just how dogs are able to enter
Sleepy Dog Land?.
Well with out getting too complicated - what happens is
this:

You will know - if you are lucky enough to have a dog living with you - or any kind of animal for that matter, as part of your family - that 'pets' are often taking short naps. Very often - a good long sleep.

Now when an animal drops off to sleep it means only one thing. It means that their spirit, or real inner self, leaves their body and travels - as fast as lightening - straight to Sleepy Dog Land.

Sleep being the only way to travel between our worlds. They will drop off to sleep, on the comfy sofa in your lounge - or anywhere they might be for that matter.Straight away they find themselves waking up in Sleepy Dog Land.

They can in fact travel back and forth whenever they like - just by going to sleep.

So when they awake back at home, it may be because they wanted to come back and give some love to their earthly two legged families. At the same time checking that everyone is okay.

Or to get some food or go for a walk.

You see the animal has to keep coming back to it's body; to keep it fit and healthy .So many reasons really. But you get the idea.

There are in fact many other lands like Sleepy Dog Land situated near by. Special places for every one of Gods creatures, born of our earth. So do not worry. You will soon learn of all those other places within the Sleepy Dog Land dimension. We will investigate together some of their wonderful adventures.

One thing dear reader to remind you. if you are reading and enjoying this book yourself. Or if you are lucky enough to have some kind person read the story to you, please remember that the rules of life - as we know them, here on earth, do not apply in Sleepy Dog Land. It is a magical place.

Benson The Dog.

You could say that Benson (or Benson The Dog as he is known) is the 'hero' of our stories. The leading man you might say.

Benson is a 'Stafford' (This is what we humans call Bensons breed) They are lovely dogs. Alert and bright and stuffed full to bursting with love. They enjoy, very much,running and jumping, and sniffing out adventures with their ever busy snouts. Stafford's are genuine, life loving dogs.

Benson is all of these things and more.

In fact Benson is rather a special dog. Which you will discover later on in this story.

Benson lives with his human family in London, England.

Benson lives with his two legger family, in a suburb of London called Greenwich.

There is a large park, and vast heathland near by. Excellent for fun and frolics.

Benson lives with his beloved, small two leggers, Jack and Sheila. These particular two leggers have been on an adventure before with Benson. They even visited Sleepy Dog Land. But that is another story.(See Tales From Sleepy Dog Land. The Crying Dog.)

So now, let's join Benson The Dog and friends..

RAGNAR'S TOOTH.
So the ancient ones say
night may soon conquer day
though our Mighty Protector still stands.
But as time passes by
he might wither and die
and the darkness will cover our land.
Then a hero must rise
blazing truth fills his eyes
with pure goodness and strength in his heart.
With a quest he must make
there's a journey to take
so Sleepy Dog Land will not fall apart.

To Ragnar's Tooth he must go
a fabled land deep below
where the black river flows to the sea.
Sacrifice must be made
for the treasure he"ll trade
granting life to The Happiness Tree.
If the tree once more stands
dark must flee from our land
as the roots of protection re-form.
Once the magic's bestowed
to satisfy ancient codes
only then Sleepy Dog Land's re-born.

Chapter One. The Weather and the Woeful.

Benson The Dog was bored!
"Bored, bored, bored !", he thought.
He lay, full stretch, in his little garden.
The sun was shining. It was a bright, and fresh Tuesday morning.
That meant he had the house, and garden all to himself.
His family of two leggers, were either at school, or at work.
Two leggers, is the name, that doggies, and all other animals have for us Humans. Perhaps, apart from chimps and apes and the like, for obvious reasons.
If you were able to read the last adventure from Sleepy Dog Land (The Crying Dog) you will already know all about Benson and his family.

Benson was deep in thought. At the same time, casually giving himself a good wash and clean. He so enjoyed this little, doggy style ritual.
"Well, it's official", Benson mused, "I am bored!"
Nothing much ever seems to happen here anymore?

In fact, Benson, actually, felt rather out of sorts? Yes indeed, he felt depressed, and under the weather.

He just could'nt understand quite why?

It had been a good three years ,in our earthly time, since Bensons last adventure. Well, the last adventure that we have heard about anyway.

Now that,of course is a lot longer in dog years.

There are,in fact, seven years of doggy time, to one year of our human time clock. So that meant Benson The Dog had aged around twenty one years.

So, Benson was no spring chicken anymore.

He had grown up.

Something is definitely going on, he thought.

But what!

Benson slowly stood to his feet. The ache in his joints was getting worse.

He padded his way, through the dog flap, and in through the front door. He smiled his Staffie grin; as he remembered how his two legger Dad had made this entrance, and exit just for him.

Seemed like such a long time ago now.

Benson made his way, carefully, up the winding stairs, and into the family apartment. He walked down the corridor,and through the kitchen, out through the glass doorway, on to the balcony.

Strange,Benson thought. I can feel something is wrong. Very wrong indeed.

He was amazed to feel the sudden change in the weather.

In the time it had taken Staffie Benson to make his way through the apartment, and out side on to the balcony, the weather had noticably changed. For the worse!

The once bright sunny sky, had, quite suddenly, seemed to develop a great deal of grey and wintery looking cloud cover.

The breeze, that before, had been light and fresh, had now become cold, damp, and biting!

The SeptemberTuesday morning, had now taken on the look and feel of a winters day in late November.

I do believe it's going to snow? thought Benson. I can feel it!

"Brrrrrr," he growled.

Benson padded back inside.

He suddenly knew he had to go back down stairs, and out into the front garden. There was something he thought he should check up on.

So back through the apartment and down the stairs he went.

"Oh dear, my limbs feel so achey and heavy", he thought.

Over the years Benson,as all dogs and animals do,noticed that his joints ached. It started off as just - some of the time. But had seemed to develop into -- most of the time!

Benson, would of course, be about nine years old now,in our two legger years. But that made him around sixty seven in doggy years.

So, some artritis was quite a natural development. But that did not help Benson feel any better. But it was not just his aching limbs that bothered him at the moment. He also felt tired, and rather sick as well.

I don't understand this he pondered.

"I am feeling weak as a small puppy?", he woofed to himself.

Once back in the garden, he trotted painfully, over to the front fence, where stood the old, familliar Yew tree.

The tree looked so sad and silent. Benson looked up at the tree. Something was definitly wrong. He could smell it!

But what was it?

Then, all of a sudden it came to him. There was not a single bird anywhere?

No sight or sound of animal life at all.?

All was so very quiet.

It was just like when a very bad storm is due. All the birds and animals tend to realise what is about to happen and take some cover.

Well before we human kind, sense anything is wrong. Also the tree did not look the same.

The yew tree was indeed an old tree. Well, at least a couple of hundred years old, when measured on the two legger time scale.

But the tree had always looked healthy and true, despite it's age.

But now, as Benson gazed up at it, the old Yew tree seemed to look every year of it's vast age.

In fact, it looked as if it were dying?

There was a definite smell about it as well. Of course only animals have this gift of such acute, and well developed senses.

The smell of dying wood seemed to get, suddenly, far more pungent and intense.

Benson had to learn more. He was getting quite worried, and agitated now.

To top it all, as he was gazing at the Yew tree, he started feeling even weaker, and very strange indeed.

As Benson was thinking these thoughts the weather completely changed.

The skies opened and it began to rain.

It rained as if it would never stop raining again!

Benson made his way inside the door, through the doggy flap. He shook himself vigerously. But as he was doing this, the strange feeling came over him again.

He started feeling sick and dizzy? Benson padded towards the stairway slowly. But suddenly a darkness came over him. He just felt he had to lay down, before he fell down!

Just as these thoughts were rushing around in his head Benson passed out - completely.

All was darkness!

Gradually, Benson awoke. He opened his eyes, and to his surprise, he found himself laying in the bluebell meadow.

Deep in the heart of Sleepy Dog Land.

"How, by the Mighty Protector, did I get here?" he thought.

All, was definitely not well. Not well at all!

You see ,as you perhaps may already know, dear reader. Normally, when an animal reaches Sleepy Dog Land, the rules in our two legger world do not apply. For instance, time is different in this magical world.

Also any aches and pains a doggy might be feeling, here on Earth, simply do not exist in Sleepy Dog Land.

At least they never had before?

As Benson stood up the first thing he felt was sick.

Also his joints burned as if they were on fire!

"I still feel awful?", he said to himself.

"Weak as a kitten and so very tired?". "I have to get to see the Mighty Protector". "He'll know what to do!"

Benson looked around to get his bearings.

He was in the bluebell meadow not far away from the woodland, where The Happiness Tree, The Mighty Protector, stood.

Benson started ,painfully trotting, over towards the vast woodlands.

As he did so, Benson started singing, to himself.

The ancient words, in praise of the Mighty Protector.

Hail 'The Happiness Tree'
In a place we all go.
With a wagging of tail
and a bright shiny nose.
Greet The Happiness Tree
he's so ancient and wise
such wisdom and truth
he will know if we've lied.

Praise the Happiness Tree
always gentle and kind
as he dries all those tears
that our lives leave behind.
He has lived here forever
see how proudly he stands
mighty wooded protector
watching over our land...

Benson made his way onward. Though, he could not
help but think, just how strange all had become in his
beloved Sleepy Dog Land.
The first thing he noticed was everything seemed so
similar, to how it had been, in the garden back home.
He could not hear or see any other animals?
There were no other doggies about? No birds flying
overhead either?
All seemed so silent and empty?
Sniff, sniffing the air, with his ever busy snout, he
couldn't help but notice
how damp and chilly the atmosphere was?
In fact, everything seemed to have become a good deal
darker. The grass, the trees, plants and foliage, seemed
to have lost their energy, and once vibrant colour.
"By the Mighty Protector, what is happening?" Benson
mused.
He was worried now. Very worried indeed.
Panting, Benson reached the edge of the woodland.
"I am, even out of breath?" he exclaimed - out loud.
Confused, and worried ,Benson padded his way through
the woodland towards the centre. To where the
Happiness Tree stood, ruling and protecting the realm of
Sleepy Dog Land.
Just as Benson reached the centre of the wood,he heard
a familliar voice.
"Benson The Dog, I wondered when you would get
here".

The growly voice was that of King the big shaggy
German Sheppard.

Benson knew King well. In fact, they had been
adventurer's together in the past. They were very good
friends indeed.

"But you don't look at all well?" continued King, as he
padded over to Benson in a concerned snouty,
sniffy,doggy kind of a greeting.
"I don't feel well!", replied Benson sadly.
"Do you know what's going on King?"
"Well no, not really?" said King.
"But I do know the Happiness Tree has summoned us
all to his counsel".
"Especially you Benson" King growled.
"Ah", said Benson. "That would explain my sudden
journey here"
"Come on Benson, we had better join the others" said
King
Benson looked anxiously at King.
"The others?" queried Benson,looking around at a silent
woodland.
"What others?"...
They padded together towards the centre of the woods.

Chapter Two. The Storm.

The school day had finished, and Jack and Sheila were
just returning home.
The weather was appalling!!
It was stormy and blustery. The time was only around
four thirty in the afternoon, but it was already dark.
Dad had collected them from school, on his way home
from work.

They all stood at the front door, while Dad fiffed and faffed ,searching through all his pockets, trying to find his door key.

"Please hurry Dad" said Jack. "We're starting to get wet!"

Sure enough, it had started raining, and raining with a vengance!

"Sorry kids, I've found it".

Dad turned his key happily, in the lock, and they pushed open the front door. All three almost falling inside.

The sight that met their eyes, made all three stand very still indeed!

There, at the bottom of the stairs, laying in a heap, was Benson The Dog.

"Benson, Benson", shouted Sheila. "What's wrong with him?"

"Let me see " said Dad."He's probably just asleep?".

Dad squatted down next to Benson stroking him.

"Come on boy " said Dad."You can't stay there".

But to their horror Benson did not awaken.

"Well he's breathing?" said an anxious Dad.

"But he's ill?" said Sheila. She was holding back the tears as she spoke.

"Now, don't panic", soothed Dad.

"Let's get him upstairs".

"Give me a hand Jack"?. "Here hold these for me?".

He gave Jack his brief case and keys.

Dad picked Benson up, and into his arms.

They carried Benson upstairs and into the apartment.

"We'll put him on the sofa in the den".

Dad carried Benson into the chilldrens play room, and placed him carefully on to the sofa.

Benson still did not awaken. He just lay on the sofa ,fast asleep.

Then they began to realise that Bensons breathing seemed rather too shallow.

"Something is wrong!" said Dad.

"I'll phone the Vet right away!"
Dad picked up the telephone and started dialling, whilst
Jack and Sheila stood by, in worried silence.....

Benson and King had reached the centre of the
woodland.
There in front of them stood The Mighty Protector.
But today, he looked like - one very unhappy -
Happiness Tree.
Grouped around the great tree, stood a countless number
of Sleepy Dog Land residents.
There was some rabbits, and birds of all descriptions.
Avia the eagle was there.
Other lands, in the magical domain, were represented.
There were, lizards,horses,donkeys, and of course cats.
Even Old Joe - the mole was there.
Many more species, too numerous to mention.
Amoungst a group of various doggies was Bounce.
Bounce had once been recscued by Benson and his
friends; on a past adventure.(The Crying Dog)
In fact, Bounce had, for a time, lived with Benson and
his two legger family. Bounce had soon found a lovely
new family of two leggers, very close to Bensons home.
"Bounce!". greeted Benson.
Bounce padded over to Benson and sniffed him and
said.
"You do not look well Benson?". Benson nodded sadly.
He really did not feel at all well.
Benson and King looked at each other.
"Dare we awaken the Mighty Protector?", woofed King.
"We have to do just that, if we are going to find out
exactly, what is going on?" replied Benson.
"The song, the ancient words!" said Benson and King in
unison.
They started to chant the ancient words...

Hail 'The Happiness Tree'
In a place we all go.

With a wagging of tail
and a bright shiny nose.
Greet The Happiness Tree
he's so ancient and wise
such wisdom and truth
he will know if we've lied.
Praise the Happiness Tree
always gentle and kind
as he dries all those tears
that our lives leave behind.
He has lived here forever
see how proudly he stands
mighty wooded protector
watching over our land...
Awaken, oh great tree..!
Awaken, for our sake's....!!

As the dogs finished chanting, the Happiness Tree
seemed to move, and gather himself up.
The familiar face of the tree appeared, in the trunk as
always.
But this time he looked different, very different indeed.
There was no smiles, or humour in his bright old eyes,
as there normally would have been.
When he spoke, his once great, and booming voice,
sounded thin and weak.
His face, and general demeanour looked; so very sad,
and listless.
"Benson, King and Bounce?, you answered my call".
"Thankyou!".
"Yes, s-sir", stammered a nervous, and increasingly tired
Benson.
King and Bounce howled respectfully, to the great tree.
"W-what is going on sir?",Benson asked.
Benson began to explain what had been happening to
him that day. Also telling the tree, just how ill he felt,
and that even in Sleepy Dog Land, his aches and pains

were still troubling him. How in fact, it was all getting worse by the minute.

There were lots of interruptions from other creatures going on as well. The whole group of worried animals, were arguing and shouting and some crying.

The Happiness Tree called for silence by shaking his branches, he shook himself so loudly - it sounded like the great storm had already arrived.

The hub-bub of noise died down, as the animals sat down, layed down, and stretched them selves, underneath the boughs of the Mighty Protector.

Every ear was pricked up, in eager anticipation, of what was about to be heard!

The Mighty Protector took a deep, and laboured breath, and began to speak...

"My dear children", began the Happiness Tree.

"I have to start by telling you all, that the situation we find ourselves in, is a very dangerous one indeed!".

"It is going to take all our strength and courage; to stop this calamity happening!"

"In fact, it threatens our very exsistance, and that of Sleepy Dog Land, and all other lands too !!"

"Long before the very birth of Sleepy Dog land, the ancient ones were at work".

"Their ancient magic created our lives, our lands, in fact our very exsistance is their doing!".

The Happiness Tree continued to explain everthing about everything, to his nervous, yet attentive group of followers.

How, and when, Sleepy Dog Land was created, and some of the reasons why.

Well, the reasons he knew about anyway. The great tree freely admitted that he did not know everything.

"I may be you leader and Lord, but, believe it or not, I too have my limits, and there are boundaries, that even I must follow!"

"There is far more mystery, and magic going on all the time, that you, or I can fully understand!!"

"I only know that the old magic, and ancient rules, must always be followed to the letter".
" Or destruction and darkness will hold sway"
."Not only bringing chaos and death to our lands here, but all other worlds, that are connected with Sleepy Dog Land ".
"Which are many, and vast !".
"So dear friends and children".
 "You must listen carefully, as your very lives - may well depend upon it !!".
The Mighty Protector continued..
It seems, that before time was even called time, there exsisted two seperate dimensions.
The dimension of the Ancient Ones, and the dimension of man.The Two Leggers.
The ancient ones, were allowed, to rule the cosmos. In effect, they were in control of all time and space.
But, as time went on, they realised that all was not well.
Their greed, and ambition, were clearly getting the better of them.
Darkness and death had arrived.
They arrived so suddenly, and began to cloud the dimensions, accompanied by storm and famine.
The only way for the ancient ones to continue, was to make drastic changes.
They must use the old magic, to create a world of immortality here, and a dimension of mortal trial.
Which we now know as Earth. Or Two Legger World.
It was felt, by the ancient ones, and those who ruled, these ancient mystical beings, because we are all ruled by others, in some way or another, that man needed help in his daily trials, and tribulations.
This course of action, it was felt, would halt the progress of the evil darkness, that was threatening to destroy their world - and their very existence.

So, Sleepy Dog Land was created. The world of immortality and magic.

The ancient ones took pleasure in creating the magical, Sleepy Dog realm.

But when it was created, it was not known as Sleepy Dog Land.

It was known then as Ragnar's Tooth.

Now, as I have said, Sleepy Dog land has existed, far longer than the world of men.

But it was not then, as we now understand it to be.

The ancients , in their wisdom, decided that man need help in his day to day life.

So animals were created. Now, this was not accomplished by the ancient ones themselves. But in fact, by a far greater, and much higher, and more mysterious power indeed.

The very first creature to become a living, breathing entity, was Ragnar.

Or, Ragnar - The Black Wolf.

Of course, the term Wolf was unheard of then.

Ragnar - was just Ragnar.

The use of the terms like, wolf and dog, bird and cat, were all names and descriptions, created by the two leggers themselves, far later in the future.

Now, Ragnar was given great power by the ancients. Power to father many,many more of his species.

In time, a length of time far too long for even us to imagine, Ragnar had sired a considerable race of followers. Each new born wolf was, in turn, given the power to sire others.

Sons and daughters etcetera. Whom in turn sired their own sons, and daughters. This went on, and on throughout the ages.

Once these creatures were born, they soon became sentient. Which means, that they understood their existence, or that they existed. Up to a point.

Now of course, as in any new society ,or old society for that matter, rules are made, and rules are taken seriously. But, as often happens - rules are also broken! Ragnar ruled his followers with heavy claw.!..

Chapter Three. The Tree Continues..

Sheila and Jack sat in silence . Benson was cradled in the childrens lap, as Dad drove them, as speedily as was safe, towards the vets surgery.
Sheila was crying,she just couldn't help herself.
"Please don't worry Sheila," said Dad.
 "I'm sure he will be fine".
"But he won't wake up?", Sheila replied, between tears.
Jack leaned over to Sheila whispering. "Come on sis, he's bound to be in Sleepy Dog Land, that's all ".
Now just to remind you dear readers. Sheila and Jack knew all about Sleepy Dog Land. In fact they had actually been there! (Tales From Sleepy Dog Land volume 1..The Crying Dog.)
But that was over three years ago, and as we all know, memories,especially at their tender ages, can become distant, and even start to feel, as if perhaps they had all been just dreams, and not reality.

"Something must be going on there?",Jack continued.
"Do you really think so Jack?", are you really sure it was all real "? Sheila replied.
"Definitely sis!", Jack assured her. "He is probably with the Happiness Tree as we speak !"
Sheila nodded nervously, all the time,stroking and comforting the sleeping Benson .
"Oh Jack, I do hope you're right"?
Dad leaned his head back, still with his eyes on the road.
"Now come on you two ".

"Enough of the games , Benson is just under the weather, he will be fine once the vet has seen him". "He will know exactly what to do!".

The children did not reply, but sat sadly, and silently, cradling Benson, as Dad drove on.

The weather was awful! It had even begun to snow now. The wind had blown up to a strong gale. The rain had turned to sleet, and then to snow.

The snow had even started to stick. Unheard of in September.

In fact, it looked more like Christmas, mid - winter, rather than Autumn.

They arrived at the vets surgery. Dad drove into the small car park ,and found a suitable spot. He turned off the engine.

"Right you two, let's get Benson into the vets office, and we had better hurry, or we'll all get soaked!".

Dad collected Benson and carried him into the vets reception.

The two children followed quickly...

While all this was happening in the world of the two leggers, the Happiness Tree continued his story...

Ragnar did indeed rule his followers with a heavy claw. But all in all he was fair with all, though very strict indeed. For the animals that broke his rules, there was no mercy shown at all.

But as time went on Ragnar became worse. Cruelty had become his very nature.

Things could not go on the way they were,or the great and dark evil that Ragnar had become, would cover the worlds, and destroy all life, good or bad.

The ancient ones were in grave mood.

Something had to be done about Ragnar.

That something was me!

They created a seed. A very special seed. They took a tooth from Ragnar himself. The tooth was one of

Ragnars front fangs. This of course did not go down well with Ragnar. But he was powerless to resist.

With this they ,don't ask me how, fashioned a seed. A seed that would transform the now dark dimension of Ragnar's tooth, into the wonderful and magical land of Sleeping Dogs. They planted the seed here. Right here in the heart of Sleepy Dog Land.

I was born.

I was created to give balance to the deep magic.

My goodness, to halt Ragnar's ever increasing evil.

Over a timeless time I grew, and my roots grew strong, spreading and covering this land with my magic.

Connecting me to every living thing.

As time continued, Ragnar's powers were curbed, and dwindled. Ragnar's followers began to evolve and change, some into different species of animal completely. Birds ,cats, and many,upon many more. So the animal kingdom was born.

But the ancients had decided that all life must be born of mortality.

Life had to start it's journey, born of the earthly dimension.

The Two Legger world.

Two Leggers were created by the higher powers. They themselves; took a great deal of time, to become as we understand them now.

The great wolves that had been Ragnar's army now played another role.

The wolves born of Earth were evolving all the time.

Helped along by two legger needs.

The two leggers became experts of interbreeding, creating many new, and varied, species. Which we know now as, dogs.

Dogs were trained, and bred, to assist the two leggers, in the different aspects of their daily lives.

Ragnar became very angry about what had become of his once proud kingdom. He cursed the ancient ones.

Ragnar swore on oath, that he would stop and destroy the ancient ones. He would return all things to the way they had been. He waged war on the ancients.

But with his powers now so weak; that he failed.

Because of his great crimes, the ancient ones banished Ragnar. They sent him back into the dark world. Deep down below, where the Black River flows to the sea. Ragnar was forced into timeless sleep.

But before this could happen, Ragnar cursed the ancient ones, and swore he would one day return, and take back what was rightly his, or destroy all lands.

He would reclaim all the things he believed to be his own.

"But surely great tree, Ragnar's Tooth is just a fable? surely a legend?" interrupted Benson.

"Ssshhh, dear Benson, you must let me continue!".

"I was created to look after the lands, and to keep you ALL safe, my dear children"

".I create the harmony, and the happiness, that we all now know as Sleepy Dog Land". "My charges include, not only our own creatures, but also all our other friends".

" All those born of Two Legger Earth!".

The Happiness Tree continued.

" Our greatest, gravest, and most immediate problem now, is that Ragnar has awoken" !

"He has awoken, and now, The Black Wolf searches for revenge!".

"He wants to take back what he truly believes is his. Either that, or destroy whatever he cannot have!".

"He is already working the old magic for his own ends".

"Hence the weather, and the strange happenings here in Sleepy Dog Land, and on planet Earth".

"We are all in a dire situation!".

"I am his first target!".

"You see, my children, with me gone, Ragnar will be able to walk abroad our lands once again!"

"Now, I have to warn you all here and now".
I am slowly dying!!".
All fell into silence, as the stunned animals, finally
started to understand what was happening. And how
serious things were.

Chapter Four. The Tree Explains.

Benson The Dog, lay on the vets table. Fast asleep.
His breathing laboured and shallow.
Dad, and the two children, stood by watching as Mr.
Moneygrabber, the vet, examined Benson thoroughly.
"How is he s-sir?", Sheila blurted out,unable to contain
her worry any longer.
"Okay Sheila, Dad said, let me deal with this".
"How, exactly is Benson, Mr. Moneygrabber?". "What
is wrong with him?"
"Hmmm", mused the vet.
"Well, Mr. Spedding, replied the vet, I'm afraid I really
cannot tell exactly, at this moment in time?"
"I will need to do various tests?"
"But, he is certainly unwell, that's for sure?"."He is, in
fact in some sort of strange coma?".
"Well, replied Dad, we must do everything possible to
get him well again!"
"I don't care how much it costs!".
The vet smiled, and immediately agreed with this.
" Yes indeed, he continued, you must not worry
unduely".
"At the moment he at least seems stable".
"Believe me, I will leave no stone unturned in my
efforts to understand exactly what the problem might
be!"
"I will just take some blood from Benson, to establish if
there is anything
sinister going on?".
Jack and Sheila shivered, as Mr. Moneygrabber took a
sample of blood from Benson, using the longest

hyperdermic needle, they had ever had the misfortune to see.

"Now, I will give you some strong vitamin tablets, and then you must take him home, and keep him warm and comfy".

"I will call to see you, at your home tomorrow, and check how Benson is doing".

"I'll send the blood to the laboratory, and we will see what we will see!"

"The results will take a few days".

"Now, as I say, please try not to worry unduly, especially you two children". "Because,It won't do Benson any good you making yourselves ill, now will it".

"Now you take him home and I will call tomorrow evening".

"Thanks Mr. Moneygrabber", said Dad.

Dad collected up Benson, and carried him back to the car.

Followed by two very sad children indeed.

There was squaking, and meeowing, a woofing, and a squeaking. In fact, there was a good deal of general panic going on,under the shadowed boughs of the Happiness Tree in Sleepy Dog Land.

The Happiness Tree called for silence!!!

"Come on now, calm down."

"All of YOU!!", his great booming voice; commanded immediate silence.

"Now, that's better, much better!"

"I understand how worried, and how frightened you all are, but it won't do us any good at all to panic!"

The Mighty Protector shook his massive bough and the leaves trembled.

The once evergreen foliage seemed now, some how old and dry.

He pulled himself up, once again, as near to his normal great height as he could, and spoke to all the Sleepy Dog landers, that lay, sat and stood around him...

"Now this is what I want you all to do!"

"You must leave this woodland now".

"You must all find shelter away from this place".

"Because here, none of you are safe!", " You must all travel , seeking refuge in the caves of the high mountains".

"If you all leave now, you should make it in time!"

"But I want Benson The Dog to stay here!.

Benson stood,painfully to his feet. He stood looking at the great tree intently.

"I have work for you Benson The Dog".

"Work only you may acheive!!".

The other animals obeyed. They all started to turn away from the tree, making their way, through the woodland toward the Sleepy Dog praire lands. Which led on to the mountainous regions.

"How can I help oh mighty protector", asked a sickly, and rather frightened Benson The Dog.

Bounce, King, and Meowla the cat queen, also waited behind with Benson
all in great anticipation?

The Mighty Protector watched sadly as his children walked, trotted, ran and hopped, off in the general direction of the mountains.

"Aah, he said, their journey is long, and not an easy one!".

"But you five, your journey is longer, and by far, more dangerous!'

The five animals looked at each other uneasily.

Benson The Dog was first to speak..

"I - we do not understand, oh Mighty Protector, is our journey different?".

"Oh yes Benson". replied the Happiness Tree. Very different indeed!".

"For it is you who must retrieve the prize, the only thing that may save us all from total destruction!!".

Jack and Sheila sat together in the den.
Benson lay sleeping on the cushion strewn sofa.
" Was Sleepy Dog Land all just some wild and fantastic dream?", whispered Sheila.
"No Sheila, of course it wasn't!" Jack replied ,slight annoyance in his voice.
"You know it wasn't!" we were there." You must remember?".
"Yes, I - I guess I do,", Sheila replied uneasily.
"But it was such a long time ago, at least three years?. "I mean, we could have dreamed it all, couldn't we?".
No way!! Absoloutely no way!", returned Jack.
Sheila continued. " Oh, poor dear Benson, just look at him",tears filling her eyes as she spoke.
"I mean, if it was all real, The Happiness Tree, all those other lands, full of dear animals? ". "If it was all real, there must be some way they can help Benson?" "He - he won't die will he?"
"I JUST COULDN'T BEAR THAT".
With that Sheila lost her emotional battle , she burst into streams of tears.
"Come on now Sis?". It"ll be alright" comforted her brother. "We'll find a way to help Benson, and see for ourselves what on Earth is happening!!"
"Just look out the window?"
The children went over to the lead patterned windows, and peered out.
It was chaos.
The rain was beating down without mercy. One could hardly see through the onslaught.
The small Yew tree in the front garden was bending and struggling under the great wind's relentless breath.
The, usually busy Greenwich high road, was almost empty of traffic. Just the occasional Police car battled it's way towards the heart of Greenwich Village.

There was no one man, woman, child or even animal
any where in sight. All that met their gaze, was the now
deserted, and weather beaten pavements.
Jack and Sheila looked at each other, both mystified.
"What is happening Jack?" said Sheila.
"It's like the end of the world!!" I'm scared!!"

The Happiness Tree sighed. A deep throaty,woody sigh.
It sounded so very sad.
He seemed to have visibley shrunk in size, since the
animals had first arrived.
His old craggy face turned sadly towards the five
friends.
"Firstly he continued, I must tell you that there is a very
good chance that none of you will be able to return here
to the woodlands!".
"And even if, by the luck of the ancient ones, all of you,
or even just one of you manages to return, it still may
not change anything. Ragnar has awoken from his
slumber!". "Now, at the moment he is still below
ground. He must still wait in the shadows. But should he
reach the surface,should he walk abroad in the now
fading light of Sleepy Dog Land, we are all doomed!".
"Not only us, but all other worlds, and life created by
the ancient ones, and even the life granted by the Great
and High Spirit of Power himself!".
"All creation will sink into the abyss of eternal darkness
and chaos!".
"But, dear children, all may yet, not be lost".

The Great and Mighty Protector continued to describe,
to a very nervous Benson and friends, all about the
quest itself.
"The five of you must leave this place,.you must take
nothing with you!".
"You will travel towards the old and fabled lands of
Ragnar's Tooth.

"The direction is out through these woodlands, and onwards towards the long praire, and eventually the Black River that flows into the great green sea".

"Your direction will be the setting sun itself!".

"You may encounter fellow travellors on route. You could find a great deal of, and sometimes surprisingly , valuble help. So always keep alert, and on your paws. You mustn't miss a thing!"

"This could make or break your mission!"

"Now listen carefully!"

"Once you arrive at the Black River, only Benson The Dog must cross the waters. Benson you must,from that point on, travel alone!

Into the dark and ancient land!!".

'It's vital you all understand this, and that all of you are completely clear on this point!"

"It is an important, and critical rule of the ancient magic"

"Benson The Dog, must go on alone!!".

"So say the words of the ancients!".

The Happiness Tree then spoke. His voice and demeanour carried a great and deep reverence...

Only one bold of heart - with truest of soul
one gifted of innocence born.
Only one strong in mind - with clearness of voice
may bless and calm the storm.
Only one made to shine no longer in prime
and has notion of fleet footed youth
Only one paying sacrifice understanding the price
bears the great cost of Black Ragnar's Tooth.

As the Mighty Protector concluded, all were stunned. They could do nothing, but sit in silence - while the words of the Happiness Tree echoed in their minds. But mostly in the mind of Benson The Dog...

CHAPTER FIVE. The Quest Begins.

Meanwhile back in Two Legger Earth, Jack and Sheila were still brooding in the den, trying to comfort a prostrate Benson.

It was nearly time for bed.

Mum and Dad had been in and out of the den checking on Benson, and telling the children not to worry, and that all would be alright.

"It's all very well Mum and Dad saying everthing will be alright?,said Jack, but they don't know what we know!".

"No I suppose not,"replied Sheila.

"But we actually don't know - do we?" she continued.

"I mean do we really know, that all this weirdness is something to do with Sleepy Dog Land?".

"It has to be!, replied her brother, I mean, what other answer could there possibly be?". "Just stop and think for a mimute Sis, It all started today, Benson being sick, the weird weather?. "All of it started happening today!".

"I mean there's real panic going on out there, It's all over the news!!"

"Night Mum , she'll be alright." said Jack as bravely as he could, and went into his bedroom and closed the door.

"In fact there's a world wide shut down going on!"

"Your right said Sheila, they don't believe we understand, they think we're too young!".

"Well, we are probably the only ones in the world who really DO understand what is going on!", exclaimed Jack.

"I'm so scared", said Sheila, shivering as she spoke. "But what can we do about it?".

Just at that moment Mum came in to the room.

"Oh come on you two, it's well past your bed time. Leave Benson to rest and sleep, so he can get well again!".

"He's not asleep!, shouted Sheila he's in a coma!!"

With that she ran into het little bedroom, slammimng
the door, and bursting into floods of tears as she did so.

The only ones left under the shade of the Happiness
Tree were Benson The Dog and his three friends,
Meowla, The Cat Queen , King and Bounce.
The Happiness Tree was first to break the loud, and
deafening silence...
" Well, it's time for you all to leave, and start your
journey!".
The four animals stood, and nrevously, started walking
towards the edge of the woodland.
"Wait for Benson at the woodland edge, continued the
Tree, I need to speak with him for a minute!".
Benson nodded to his friends and turned back to the
Mighty Protector.
"Yes sir", said Benson, pricking up his Staffie ears.
"Sit down in front of me for a moment my good doggy",
said the Happiness Tree quietly.
Benson wagged his tail, and did as he was asked, his
head to one side, he listened intently.
"Now, I think you have a good idea already how all this
is going to turn out?" "Is that not so, Benson The Dog?"
"Well sir, replied Benson. "I sort of feel like I do, but
without knowing the answer?" "If that makes any sense
sir?".
"Perfect sense for doggys Benson, but do elaborate for
me?" smiled the tree.
"Well, I feel as though once we have made the journey
to Ragnar's Tooth, things might be alright eventually,
but also I feel as if this might be MY very last journey!"
"I can't help feeling as though I might not be returning
to Sleepy Dog Land again?, and that things will never
be the same for me again?"
"I am so very, very scared - oh Mighty Protector!!".
Benson was visibly shaking as he finished speaking.
"You are indeed a wise dog Benson, replied the tree.

"Am I a coward?, I am sorry to be a coward sir, but I am so scared and troubled - and I feel awful!".
"Benson The Dog ", said the Mighty Protector, raising himself to his full height and majesty. "You are NO coward, You have been chosen to lead this quest because it is your birth right!"
"You were created - you were born to make this quest. "It was written by the ancient ones themselves."
"Did they know, all that time ago, that all this was going to happen?", replied Benson .
"Oh yes my dear son - oh yes indeed!", said the tree gravely.
"But if they knew why did'nt they stop it all?", exclaimed Benson.
"Because it has to happen this way", said the tree.
"But will we be alright?, asked Benson, will my friends be alright?".
"Benson, all I can tell you is, there will be casualties".
"I can tell you no more!" "At least no more of the eventual conclusion of this quest, only that whatever happens,Benson The Dog, I will always be with you!".
"You must be patient,he continued, you must trust in me, and the old magic!"
"But most of all Benson The Dog, you must trust in yourself - and your destiny!!".
"Now,stay a little longer, I must explain some things to you, but remember this is for your ears only! ".
Benson sat patiently on his haunches grinny panting, as Staffies do,. He sat in homage of the Happiness Tree, his big head to one side, and his ears upright.
HE LISTENED!!!

You will learn ,dear reader, just what was said as the adventure progresses.
The three friends all waitied in nervously for Benson to make an appearance..
King was scratching, Bounce was rolling about and Meowla was, doing what cats do, haughtily.

They were trying to get shelter under some bushes.
The weather was worsening in rapid fashion.
"Oh dear, she muelled, will he be much longer do you suppose?"
"Are you talking to me cat queen?" growled King.
Between you and me readers,King did not really like cats. Even though, as we know, in Sleepy Dog Land there is none of the distrust and fear, that dogs and cats have for each other, when on Two Legger Earth.
It was the weather and the magic breaking down that was causing Kings animosity and resentment..
"Well really!" meowed Meowla.
"Do you have to be so very rude? you great shaggy brute?"
King appologised.
"He won't be long now, I can sense he's on his way!".
Bounced wagged and jumped about in excitiment..
"OOh goody, he barked, I can't wait to get going, we'll make everything better- won't we King?"
"We will do our best Bounce". "We can only do our best!", replied King.
Just as King had finished speaking, Benson appeared, limping out of the undergrowth.
"Okay then, he said, are we all here?".
Two barks and a purr answered his question.
"What did he say, what did the great tree say, asked a very sqeaky, and over excited Bounce. Westies are very excitable.
"Nothing to worry you Bounce," said Benson.
"Let's get started then!", he continued.
The three friends turned towards the praries, and started walking.
But they hadn't taken a few steps when they heard a small voice behind them.
"Oy."
"OYYY, WAIT OOP!!!".

They stopped ,and turned around to see, what, or whom
was making the strange greeting.
It was Old Joe Mole.
Oh" what?", exclaimed King.
"What are you doing here Moley, you should be
burrowing your way to the mountain retreats, with all
the others".
"I'm coooming with thee three!" said the small animal.

Let me just explain readers.
Old Joe Mole is of course a mole. A small burrower of
good repute.
He is from the north of England, on Two Legger World,
hence his rather unique accent. But he has lived in
Sleepy Dog Land for longer than any other resident
actually knows. He has, kind of always been there, as
far as anyone really remembers.
I know what you are thinking. If Old Joe Mole, is a
mole, then what is he doing living in Sleepy Dog Land?
He should be across the great Green Sea in Molehaven
(The mole equivalent of Slleepy Dog Land)
Well, the thing about it is this.
Old Joe Mole is actually convinced he's a dog!
Yes, you read me correctly. He has,as far as he is
concerned, always been a dog. He doesn't get on very
well with Moles. Because, he is forever chasing them.
So in the end he was banished from Molehaven.

"Oh for the great tree's sake!?", growled King.
"There's no way he can come with us??". It'll take
forever with moley features tagging along!"
"Besides, he's weird!".
Benson interupted.
"No King, I knew Joe Mole was coming with us, the
great tree told me earlier".
"We are going to need his talents?"
"OH What?, but just look at those little steps he takes?",
King exlcaimed.

"Eeeeh by goom ya big blatherer' Joe woofed (yes he woofed the words. Well as I said, he does believe he's a dog)

" I can reed on thee's back! ,Yer big an oogly eenough, ain't thee?".

Before King could complain Benson said...

"Yes indeed King, that's what to do, he can ride on your back most of the way?"

"You've no problem with that have you?".

"Well no, I suppose not", said King, rather crossly. "If you say so Benson!, if you say so..!".

"Come on then, up here with you, Old moley face!!".

"Dooon't yee call me moley face! exclaimed Old Joe, firstly, I am neet a mole, I am ah dog , and secondly, i'm neet weird!!!"

"Oh, fine", replied King, "Just get aboard my back!".

Old Joe tried a few times to clamber up on to the great shaggy dogs back but simply kept slipping off again, King's height just to much for his little legs to cope with.

"Oh for the grace of the tree!! woofed a bad tempered King.

"Here I'll do it!!"

With that King lent down and got his big snout under Old Joe Mole, flipping the little creature over his big head.

Joe landed safely, holding on tightly to pawfuls Kings long and soft chestnut hair.

"Thur we goo!, he barked excitiedly (a very odd sound indeed) let's geet gooing!!"

King sighed, the other three, laughed and laughed.

"He's right",said Benson The Dog.

"Let us be on our way, the quest has begun!!".

So our five friends departed. They must have looked a strange group.

Benson taking the lead.

Meowla,and Bounce trotting together just behind the Staffie.

While King, with Old Joe (doggy) Mole riding on his back,brought up the rear of the group.

The five ,would be, adventurers, turned their heads away from the comforting woodland foliage, and made their way towards, the now desolate, and wind swept praire lands of Sleepy Dog Land.

In the direction of a red, and setting sun.

On their way towards those dark - those fabled lands.

Those dreaded, and barren lands.

Towards the land, they all, now knew as - Ragnar's Tooth.....

CHAPTER SIX. The Journey.

Back on Two Legger Earth...

There was no way that Sheila felt she would be able to sleep.

She was far too upset, what with all that was going on.

But, as always happens, sleep finally won the battle, and she eventually dropped off.

Jack was in the same situation.

He just couldn't turn his brain off. His mind was racing and desperately trying to analise what was going on around him?

The sudden storms? The desolation that followed. All this seemed to be taking over his happy home.

Benson,very ill, and in a coma?

He just knew that it all had to be, to do with Sleepy Dog Land!

Remember readers, that Jack and Sheila had a lot of experience with Sleepy Dog Land.

They had , once a upon a time, actually been there!!..

How could he get to the bottom of it all.

Find the answers?

But, as with Sheila , a worried exhaustion overcame him, and sleep finally kicked in....

The four companions were making their way through the wind swept, and very stormy praire lands.

Benson was leading the way..

Travelling for a good eight hours ,in earth time,they had come upon a great rocky area, at the foothills of the eastern mountains.

"Hold up a minute!", panted Benson The Dog.

"Perhaps we might rest here for a while, and get our bearings?".

"I'm with you!", growled King.

The four trotted over to a small cave, just beneath, a smal moss covered hill.

It was sheltered, to a point - and would provide some sort of cover from the raging bluster - of the never ending storms.

They were all now, tired, wet and very cold indeed.

"Come on let's get under cover!", barked Benson.

They entered the small cave.

It was dry, and surprisingly warm.

Meowla was first inside, straight away finding a small rock shelf, which she climbed at speed , as cats do, and sat cleaning herself, all the time looking around haughtily.

The rest of the group followed her in, and settled in a small circle.

Benson was the first to speak.

"Well, we've come this far",he said.

"Now I think it's time to tell you a little bit more of what is to befall us".

There was a sadness in Benson's voice as he spoke.

This did not go unoticed by his companions. They sat listening intently.

The Happiness Tree stood. He was sad, and troubled. His thoughts distant.

Once the five adventurers had departed, he had raised himself to his full great height. Standing and watching over a now, desolate and barren Sleepy Dog Land. Strectching his great life giving roots, just as far as he could manage. But it was getting harder all the time. As the light was fading, so was his great strength.

The time is soon! he thought to himself.

He knew that things would never be the same again. Whatever the conclusion to all this mayhem.

The time was coming. The time of change.

The Time Of The Wolf..!!

The storm billowed and raged around him. He battled to stand firm.

For after all. He was The Mighty Protector. It was his duty.

A duty bestowed upon him in ancient times.

Bestowed upon him by ancient magic.

Magic that now wanted repayment!

The sky was dark.

Another thought, however was playing on his mind.

The two legger children, he thought. Benson The Dog's earthly friends.

They would become part of all this. They would play a role in this. That is if Two Legger Earth was to be saved!!

But just what that role was, he couldn't remember?. He just couldn't remember, however hard he tried!!

He must, somehow contact them. They had a prize. A gift given to them on their last adventure , many, many earth years ago! (Book 1. The Crying Dog)

Part of the ancient magic.

He put every ounce of his, fast fading strength, into his thoughts.

He concentrated..!!

Using what little magic he had left, he stretched his great roots out, and away - towards the two legger dimension....

Jack awoke to find Sheila sitting on the edge of his
bed..!
He wiped his eyes and yawned.
"Sis?"
"What is it Sis?"
He could see Sheila had been doing a lot of crying.
"Jack, it's worse out there, I mean it's really, really bad
now"
"Mum and Dad have only just gone to bed!".
"I heard them talking, Mum was crying?"
"We must try and do something!," urged Sheila.
"I know",said Jack.
"It's strange Sheila, but I may have some sort of an
answer?".
Jack got out of his bed and walked across his bedroom
to his wardrobe.
Dragging the small bedside chair with him. Placing the
chair next to the wardrobe, he climbed up and started
searching on the top.
"What are you doing?", asked a bemused Sheila.
"Just a minute, replied Jack. "I think I have it?..yep, here
it is!"
"Here's what?" asked his sister..
Jack climbed down off the chair, carrying a small metal
money box with him
"Here's this!"
He sat next to Sheila on the bed, putting the little box
down, on the bed between them.
Sheila watched as Jack opened the box. There inside
was something wrapped in some kitchen foil.
Jack took out the parcel carefully.
"OUCH!!", Jack exclaimed, and quickly dropped the
mysterious pakage back on the bed.
"It's vibrating!!!, said a shocked Jack. "Sheila looked at
him?
"What?". She reach her hand slowly toward the silver
parcel and quickly touched it with her finger.

"Ooh ,Y-YES It , kind of tickles?"she said.

"But it feels somehow safe!!".

"What's in it Jack?!!".

Jack gentley picked up the strange object, and began to unwrap it.

He pulled off the foil to reveal a small piece of tree bark, shaped rather like a key?

"It's the wooden key!", Jack proudly announced.

"And it's warm?".

"Look!", said Sheila. "Look at it Jack!".

Jack held the key up, it was actually giving, a faint, warm and green glow!

"This proves it!", exclaimed Jack.

"All this going on?,it has everything to do with Sleepy Dog Land.

"But what are we to do with it now?" asked a puzzled Sheila.

Jack held the key reverently in his hands.

"Let's see?". "Come on Sis, quietly though, we mustn't wake up Mum and Dad".

They silently went out of Jack's bedroom and into the Den.

They walked carefully over to the sofa, where lay the sleeping Benson.

Sheila stood watching as Jack knelt down and placed the key carefully next to Benson's head.

They watched and waitied to see what would happen. But nothing did?.

But, the wooden key was still faintly glowing.

"I know, whispered Jack, the words - do you remember the special words?".

"Um?, what words Jack!", asked a still puzzled Sheila.

The words they always chanted; to awaken the Happiness Tree?

"I - Ithink so?", replied Sheila.

"Let's try ,said Jack, both together!"

"Ok replied Sheila, but quietly".

So they both stood up in front of Benson and the key,
and quietly chanted the ancient words..
(Why don't you read the words allowed with Jack and
Sheila , dear reader?)

Hail 'The Happiness Tree'
In a place we all go.
With a wagging of tail
and a bright shiny nose.
Greet The Happiness Tree
he's so ancient and wise
such wisdom and truth
he will know if we've lied.
Praise the Happiness Tree
always gentle and kind
as he dries all those tears
that our lives leave behind.
He has lived here forever
see how proudly he stands
mighty wooded protector
watching over our land...
Awaken great tree
Awaken for our sakes..

Jack and Sheila finished the chant, and stood back and
watched
Benson.
But Benson still lay, quietly asleep.
"Nothing's happening, said Sheila sadly"..."Nothing is
happening at all Jack?"
"Give it some time Sis, replied Jack.
"Just give the magic time to work?"
The two children sat next to Benson.
Watching and waiting.
Waiting and watching....

Benson was speaking to his friends in the little cave.

"This is where things will start to get dangerous, we are getting close, close to the fabled lands , somewhere just over the eastern mountains,I know because I can feel it!". "I CAN SENSE IT!".

"I will understand completely if anyone does not feel that they want to continue on this quest!!".

"The Great Tree says I have to go, but I have to go anyway - only I must cross the Black River".

"Only one, must cross the Black River into Ragnar's Tooth!".

"It is wriiten, that I am the one that must do this!"

"GRRRRR, No way Benson!", GROWLED King.

"I am with you all the way to the Black River. I will cross with you if you need me?"

"That goes for all of us!", the other animals shouted as one!.

"All for one, and one for all!".

Benson looked round at all his friends.There were tears in his deep brown eyes as he spoke.

"Well, Thankyou all, dear ,dear friends!".

"Then let us all continue on, and face - whatever fate, and the ancient ones have in store!!

"Oooh - eh - oop!, and off we go, arreeeet - woof eee by goom - woof". applauded Old Joe Mole.

"Oh for the great trees sake!". "Just get on my back!" , growled King. But his gruff voice was filled with admiration, and amusement, at Old Joes brave words.

The five heros walked to the mouth of the cave, and prepared themselves for the rage of the storm, and all that may await them.

As they walked out into the open air, a grim feeling, at once overtook all of them.

For all was pitch dark! There was no glowing moon whatsoever.No stars to light their way. All was darker than darkness itself.

"By the Great Tree, exclaimed a squeaky Bounce, it's all dark, and it should be dawn by now?". He woofed and started chasing his tail.

All four then stood together.

They felt a deep, deep fear.

"The red sun has now turned black!", said Benson The Dog.

"The ancient words tell of the great darkness - and the black sun!".

"Well, my friends, It is now official!!"

"We must head on, and quickly!"

"The Black Wolf has broken his bonds, released of his shackles!"

"There is little time!!".

"Ragnar - now - walks our land!!!".

CHAPTER SEVEN.   The Huffenuffs.

I would just like to take this opportunity to do a little explaining to you all, my dear readers.

If you have not read, or been told about Sleepy Dog Land before. You may be a little confused.

Now, as you are reading, and following this story. You are hearing about Benson The Dog, and his friends, on their dangerous quest in Sleepy Dog Land. Yet at the same time, you are also hearing about Benson at home with Jack and Sheila.

Well, yes. It is the same Dog. Benson The Dog.

But the Benson in Sleepy Dog land is in fact the inner self, or soul of Benson.

That part of Benson, and of course all pets, that travel to Sleepy Dog Land, and other magical lands, when they sleep.

As the poem explains:

When our dogs take a nap so their spirits take flight straight to Sleepy Dog Land
anytime - day or night.

Safe in Sleepy Dog Land
where all dogs may roam free
or hangout with their mates
"neath The Happiness Tree.
Tasty treats there aplenty
lushous grass just to chew
anything they could want for
every wish will come true.
Such a magical haven
where no dog has a care
It's a realm of true wonder
In amidst of a prayer.

I do hope that answers some questions for you all!
Now back to the story...

Sleep must have overtaken the two children. Because
the next thing they knew Mum was calling to them to
get up.
"No way!" , said Jack.
"No way am I going to school today with Benson like
this!"
But Mum was not calling them for school.
"She entered the room and sounded very upset and
worried indeed!
"There's no school today kids!", everything is on shut
down".
"We can not go out of our homes, the police are telling
everyone, and it's all over the news!!".
They looked out of the window.
The storm raged on!! High winds, hail and snow were
also forcast.
"Now how is Benson?, asked Mum, walking over to the
sofa.
"He's just the same replied Jack.
"Well Mr. Moneygrabber, the vet is due this morning.
Perhaps his tests will shed some light on all this?".
Jack and Sheila looked at each other nervously.

"Now come and get some breakfast inside you, we are all going to need our strength!".

 With that Mum left the den, the children followed. Jack putting the faintly glowing, wooden key safely into his pocket.

They followed Mum into the kitchen where they all sat down to breakfast.

But no one was really very hungry?

Benson and friends marched on.

It was darker than dark and the great winds were echoing through the rocks and crevices.

Old Joe Mole was riding on the great shaggy German Sheppards back, and singing away.

Much to Kings obvious annoyance, yet also with his quiet admiration of this little chaps courage!

Away we all go
but to what we don't know.
Four soldiers and heros alike.
Three dogs and a cat
tell me how's about that
We are all going to do what is right!!

Of course this was sung at the top of his sqeaky little voice,

and in his, unique northern accent,as he jumped up and down on Kings shaggy back!

"That just has to be enough! complained King!

"You really are giving me a headache!"."Not to mention a sore back!!"

"Oh come on now King,", soothed Benson.

"Be nice to him., it's just his way of dealing with all this".

King nodded his big head.

"Yes indeed Benson", he replied.

"He certainly is a gutsy little chap!".

Old Joe, fairly glowed at King's comment.

They wandered on ,all deep in their own thoughts.
Meowla was thinking about how much she was missing
her family and friends in Puurland.
She had been away from home now, for, what seemed
like, a very long time. In fact she couldn't remember just
how long it had been since The Happiness Tree had
called her to Sleepy Dog Land. But it was, just about
when the storms had started. She had been needed. So
she came! Unusual for a cat. But Meowla really wasn't
like other cats, she ,mostly, thought of others before
herself.
Bounce was trying not to think about things too much.
He found it better just to get on with everything , and
take whatever came his way, and deal with it. He was
very scared, but promised himself he wouldn't show it
too much. He felt safe with Benson and King at his
side.Bounce was a brave little doggy at heart. Westies
are a tough breed!
King was worried! Not so much for himself but for his
friends. Especially Benson.
Benson did not look at all well. And as the storms got
worse he could see that the brave Stafford, seemed to
become weaker, as if in harmony with the terrible
weather! He must assist Benson all that he could, and of
course his new friends, and brothers in arms...
Still deep in thought, King suddenly heard a hissing and
spitting!
It was Meowla..
"Hold up"! she ordered. "Everyone stop and listen!".
They all did as she asked. Eight pairs of doggy ears
procked up and listened intently. Well eight pairs if you
count Old Joe Mole?. Which of course is only fair!
There was a sort of whispering sound going on near by?
"Just behind those rocks and bracken?", urged Meowla.
Old Joe leapt from Kings back, his tiny fists balled and
ready for action.

It would have set them all into laughter, if they hadn't been so scared.

"I hear it now!", growled King.

All five looked towards the rocky bracken.

Just then there was a loud whooping and banging of a drum?

"What, in The Great Tree's name is going on? ,challenged Benson.

All of a sudden there was whispering, and loud drum banging, all around the group of friends.

They turned this way, and that, trying see what was happening.

Then they saw!

Out of the darkness and mist ,all around them now, they could just make out the shapes of what looked like two leggers?. Very small two leggers!

About half the size of the usual two legged man.

They all carried weapons and drums.

Some were brandishing little axes, whilst the others were banging their small drums - for all they were worth!

"WHOAA THERE..!!!", came a small, gruff but strong voice.

"WHOAA I SAY..!!!".

Benson, King , Bouce and even Old Joe stood firm! Growling and barking fiercely. Meowla's fur was standing on end like small pine needles. She hissed and spat at the small men!!

They were surrounded.

Jack and Sheila stood in the doorway of the den. Watching what was going on.

Mr. Moneygrabber, the vet, had arrived a little after breakfast. He was knelt down by the sofa examining Benson The Dog.

"Hmmm!", he pondered.

"Well?, Mr. Moneygrabber?",said Dad. He had the trace of a smile on his lips as he spoke.

Dad could not help smiling, even with all this mayhem going on. He had said in the past how suitable Mr. Moneygrabber's name was. How it was perfect for a vet. Because we all know how expensive vet are!

Dad continued speaking.

"What's the verdict?". "Have you any idea what is wrong with Benson?".

"Well, not as such?," replied the vet.

"He is definitely comatose however." "The thing is, there seems no physical reason for it? Apart from signs of arthritus,Benson seems phsycally fit!".

"His blood tests came back negative, we could find no signs of disease?".

"But the main problem is - he is getting weaker all the time!".

"This is odd, to say the least!"

"When was the last time Benson ate?".

""Yesterday morning," replied Dad.

"Well unless he comes round in the next day or so,continued Mr. Moneygrabber, we are going to have to feed him through a tube!"

"That can work out as very expensive indeed!".

"No problem , money wise relpied Dad.

Mr. Moneygrabber, seemed to noticably perk up, as soon as money was mentioned.

He stood up and with a beaming smile said..

"Well let's leave it a day, see if Benson comes round. If, however there is no change. I am afraid we will have to consider other options".

"Call me in the morning Mr. Spedding".

With that, he shook Dad firmly by the hand, and disappeared out of the den, and down the stairs, where Mum showed him out into the stormy garden.

"We will watch Benson for as long as it takes,"said Sheila.

"Okay, you two, I will leave you both in charge".

"Do call me straight away if there is any change at all.!".

Dad left Jack and Sheila with Benson, and closed the den door quietly behind him.

"Tonight Sheila, said Jack, tonight we will try the wooden key.

It is the only thing we have left".

"Perhaps there is a little magic left inside the key.

Enough for us to some how contact The Happiness Tree himself?".

"Only he can save Benson".

"Yes, agreed Sheila, and perhaps tell us what is going on?".

The two children sat next to Benson waiting for the night to arrive.

Meowla was spitting, hissing and cursing fiercely, at the strange beings that surrounded the five friends.

King was growling, so loudly that it sounded like, the already deafening thunder that was ringing out - in the dark wet skies of Sleepy Dog Land.

Bounce was a woofin' and a waffin', Old Joe was,surprisingly still singing,and hanging on to Kings hind leg for all he was worth.!!

Then Benson howled!!!

"QUIIEET!!!", howled the Staffie.

Benson was standing firm, in the centre of all this utter mayhem. His four paws firmly on the ground, his full Stafford's chest pushed out to twice it's normal size. He howled a fearsome howl!!

"Quiet, ya know - quiet - quiet QUIEEETT!!"..

All suddenly became silent. Ther drums stopped banging, King and the others stopped immediately.

For a moment all was very still.

Even the raging storm seemed to have obeyed the Staffies howl.

Then just as Benson was going to say some thing, a huge twine and metal net dropped over our five hero's.

"Whaa.!!",..exclaimed Benson.

They all tried desperately to shake the net off. But it was too heavy and tangled. It held them firmly.

They were well and truly trapped. Helpless!

Once they had all stopped squirming and biting, clawing and chewing at the net, they realised just what a true predicament they were actually in.

Benson and friends looked around, and began surveying their captors.

Benson's jaw dropped open in amazement. He had never seen the like of these strange creatures before.

Such an odd sight met his gaze..

Out of the darkness and mist, slowly walked their captors.

They were certainly similar to the Two Leggers, in that they had two legs ,two arms and walked upright.

But, there is where the similarity ended.

They were about half the height of your normal two legger, and seemed much wider.

They had long scraggy hair, that grew in wild abundance on their heads, hands, and bare feet. Their hands and feet; were dog like paws, with sharp looking claws, where one would expect nails to be. From their brow's, on either side, grew two small horn like things.

Their ears were also, kind of dog like, well more ancient wolf like really.

They wore dark brown tunics, with a thick leather belts. In the belts they carried a small axe like weapon.

The five stared in amazement.

One, whom looked like he might well be the leader moved closer, sort of sniffing at our five friends, in a very doggy fashion?

King gave him a deep throaty, but quiet, warning growl. In a deep gruff voice, that sounded very canine indeed - the leader spoke..

"Well, now we have you!".

"You are to come with us, by our master's command.
You must bow in his presence!".The strange creature
continued.
"He knew five would be coming, he said five would be
on their way!".
"He told us to capture the five, and bring,all of you to
him!"
"He wants you!!".
"We do our masters bidding!".
King inturupted - "We bow to no one!!". He growled
with such menace that Benson, quickly, broke in.." Wait
a minute here!!", who, and what are you creatures?".
"With whom am I speaking?".
The creature came slowly towards Benson, and stood so
close, that Benson could smell his dark,dank breath.
"I am Arimus of Huff!".
"I am leader of Huff's, and prime soldier to my master!".
"Huff's?,queried Benson. "What by The Great Tree are
Huff's.
Bounce interpupted.."OOOH DEAR, he woofed "They
are Huffenuffs!"..
"Don't be foolish young Bounce!" exclaimed King.
Huffenuffs are an old wives tale?" , tales mothers use to
keep their young pups in order!",they don't really
exsist?".
Old Joe interupted this time.
I know about Huffenuffs", he squeaked.
Joe then proceeded to sing the old song..

Now if you are rude
or puppy selfish or gruff
you may well turn into
a rough Huffenuff!
You will shrink half your sife
become wrinkled and tough
live the rest of your life
in one gigantic huff !!!
So remember these words

so dear puppy of mine
be willing and helpful
pleasent and kind.
To sulk and have tantrums
it's never enough
or you'll spend all your time
as an old Huffenuff..!!!

He stood back proudly.
Arimis of Huff, stamped his feet and thumped his axe
into the ground.
"We are far more than any old mothers tale", he snorted.
"We are the chosen few of The Mighty Ragnar!".
At the mention of the name Ragnar, the thunder broke
out again as if in vengance!
"I see!", said Benson, trying his best to stay calm.
"So Ragnar has sent you, Huffenuffs, to capture us five,
and you are to deliver us to him?".
"That is our mission", grumped Arimis.
"Now, will you come with us quietly?,or must we chain
and drag you?
"You just try it!!", growled King, bearing his ,more than
large teeth.
"It's alright King,said Benson, that is the route we are
quested to travel, and Ragnar is our destination.
"We will walk with you Huffenuffs - quietly!".
"Let it be so!!".Arimis ordered.
At his words, the band of Huffenuffs gathered round the
five friends, and removed the big net. With Benson the
Dog at the front, and Bounce, Meowla, King, and Old
Joe Mole,now once again riding on King's back,
followed in quiet contemplation.
Arimis walked along side Benson, and the rest of the
Huffenuffs walked beside, and behind the group of
friends, axes in hands, all on their way towards, the
fabled lair of The Black Wolf himself.
Ragnar

CHAPTER EIGHT.   The Black Wolf.

The Happiness Tree shook his boughs and branches.
Leaves were falling and he was feeling weaker than
ever.
He was dying. He knew this.
He had been spending his time following Benson and
his friend's progress on their way to the Black River.
So, thought the tree. They have been captured.
He knew they would be eventually. The slaves of the
Black Wolf have the five.
They are taking them to Ragnar's lair.
He was so very sad!!
He knew the trials and tribulations that they would, one
and all, have to go through - especially Benson The
Dog.
But it was written, it was their destiny being played out.
As the ancient ones had decreed, all those many, many
moons ago into the distant past.
The weaker he got, the harder he tried to project his
magic towards the Two Legger world.
He knew also, that the two children had an important
role to play in all this.
He just had to reach them.
He projected his thoughts still further, and further into
the cosmos of the Two Legger's Earth dimension.

The two children had been watching Benson all day.
They had been chanting the ancient words so many
times.They knew the poem backwards.
They had been granted very little sleep the night before.
So, of course sleep had found the two children during
the dark afternoon.
They had both fallen into deep sleep right there in the
den, next to Benson.
Jack opened his eyes. All was very quiet. He could see
Sheila curled up next to him on the floor.

All was indeed quiet. It seemed that the terrible storms
had blown themselves out, and were now resting to
gather strength, for their next terrible onslaught!.
Then Jack had a horrible shock!
He had turned to look how Benson was. But the sofa
was empty!! No Benson to be seen!!
"Oh my God!", Jack blurted out!
"Where is he?".
He shook, the still sleeping Sheila.
"Sis, sis, wake up!".
Sheila opened her sleepy eyes."W-what is it Jack?
Then she saw the empty sofa.."Oh - no!!"...She was just
about to speak when they heard a voice behind them.
"Do not be scared, my two children!!"
Jack and Sheila truned slowly around.
There, by the window - stood Benson The Dog!!
"Benson, Benson, you're alright?
"But how.."
"Ssssh now dear ones!".
As the children looked at Benson, they could see all was
not quite right.
Benson looked a lot larger than normal. His whole form
was, sort of, 'shimmering'?. He seemed to be changing
from Benson the dog into, into another shape
completely. A Tree, kind of shape?
"What is happening, Sheila stammered.
She and her brother were trembling with fear!
"Benson?"
"Be still my chilldren. You are both dreaming."
"I use Benson's form to guide you. I will explain all I
can to you both."
"Please follow me, quickly. There is very little time!"
With that, the dream Benson, turned and left the den.
The two children followed the dog , down the stairs, and
out of the open front door - into the small garden.
All was pitch black outside, apart from the small Yew
tree in the corner of the garden. The tree seemed to be

55

giving out a strange green glow, which lighted it up, as though a spot light was shining down on it from the dark, starless night sky.

The dream Benson trotted over to the tree, and sat on his haunches, bathed in the green glow of the Yew tree.

But the Yew tree had started looking less like the Yew tree and seemed to be changing into something else? It seemed bigger, wider, and so very much taller!.

"T-The Happiness Tree?" Jack stammered out the question.

The dream Benson nodded his great Staffie head in agreement. He spoke.

"Now chant the ancient words - one more time!".

Jack and Sheila did as he asked:

Hail 'The Happiness Tree'
In a place we all go.
With a wagging of tail
and a bright shiny nose.
Greet The Happiness Tree
he's so ancient and wise
such wisdom and truth
he will know if we've lied.
Praise the Happiness Tree
always gentle and kind
as he dries all those tears
that our lives leave behind.
He has lived here forever
see how proudly he stands
mighty wooded protector
watching over our land...
Awaken great tree
Awaken for our sakes..

As the children finished the words, there began much movement and rustling.

The small Yew tree was no longer small, but huge and towering. Growing up, and up - into the pitch black of the night sky.

The green glow became brighter and brighter almost blinding the two children. It seemed like, suddenly, the whole City of London shone.

Bathed in the bright, and magical green light!.

The large, craggy and kindly face began to appear; within the great trunk.

Until, there stood ,the Great Tree himself!. The Mighty Protector of Sleepy Dog Land, basking, in all his breath taking majesty. Before them stood - The Happiness Tree.

The two children, understandably, were speechless!

The dream Benson was no longer there. The Mighty Protector stood alone in front of the two children.

"Now, be of no fear, my small trwo legger friends!", boomed the great tree.

"Oh, thank you Great Tree, sobbed Sheila, we are both so very worried. Benson is very sick, and the weather has changed and all has gone mad here!!!" Sheila blurted this out all at once,collapsing into floods of tears.

"Can you tell us what is happening?", her brother finished.

"Yes, dear ones, to a point I can.?"

" Benson is indeed in dire peril.!".

"In fact we all are in Sleepy Dog Land.!!".

"But first, you have the wooden Key Jack?"said the tree.

"Y-Yes sir I do!" answered Jack. He took the wooden Key out of his pocket.

It glowed brightly, and kind of, pulsed in his hand. He held it up to the tree.

"That key will become very important soon,young ones", continued the tree.

"I will tell you what to do with it in time. But first let me try and explain to you both what is going on. Above the stars in Sleepy Dog Land, and sadly here on Two Legger world!".

The Happiness Tree proceeded to describe in deatil all about, Sleepy Dog Land's dilema. The quest, and, of course about The Black Wolf himself.

Ragnar.

"And that is all I can tell you now", finished the tree. "Only that your help will prove crucial to all life, in Sleepy Dog Land, and here in two legger world!".

"Now, about the key, continued the tree.

"At precisely Midnight, in your two legger time, Jack you must come here to the yew tree. You must brave the storm, and you must wait.! Wait, untill the crashing bright light strikes the yew tree. Then you must bury the wooden key beneath the earth, so it touches the very roots of the tree.

"Then you must go back and join your sister and stay with Benson!"

"He will need you!".

"Will Benson be alirght sir?" sobbed Sheila.

"That, dear one, I can not say!"

"All I can tell you is this, you both must have faith. Even though he may not show it, Benson The Dog will need you!!".

"Now brave children, you must go back, my magic is no longer strong, I can not keep this illusion going any further. I too must return, and face my given destiny!!".

"Remember, have faith, and be strong!!"

"Now go!".

With that Jack and Sheila turned away from the tree, and walked silently, through the open door, and back into their brightly lit home.

Suddenly they were back upstairs, in the den, sitting next to the sleeping Benson.

"Are we awake now Jack?" asked Sheila.

"Jack gave himself a good pinch!

"Ouch!!"..."Yes ,I'm certain of that Sis!"

"Quick have a look outside the window.
They rushed over to the window and looked outside.
The storms raged, all was wind , rain and now snow?
All was deserted in the streets below. They looked down at the Yew tree.
It stood, as it always did. Small, and rather sad looking.
Jack sat down next to the window, whilst Sheila went back and sat down next to Benson. Cradleing his big head in her arms.
Neither spoke. They sat together in silent thought.

A long, long way away, another dimension away in fact, someone else was also deep in thought.
The Balck wolf, Ragnar, padded and paced, over the cold grey rocks of the fabled lands.
His deep red eyes glowed. They glowed like the red hot coals - deep in the depths of a burning fire.
They were close now. Captured and close. Soon, very soon, he would once again,rule over all the lands of Sleepy Dog World.
He knew the ancient magic. He was the ancient magic!!!.
No one would be able to stop him. Not this time.
He smiled to himself. His great long fangs appeared over his lips as he did so.
His eyes burned deeply with anger, as he felt the gap where his missing tooth used to be. The tooth, the ancient ones had stolen. His tooth!. Used to create that tree,and it's wretched children. Used to keep him prisoner beneath the ground for so very long.
Well not this time!!
HE WAS BACK!. Back to stay!!
As he mused on all of this, Ragnar - The Black Wolf raised himself up, and on to his hind legs, threw his great head back, and howled. A howl so long, so loud, and so very awful, it could turn blood to cold ice !!

Benson trudged on. His joints felt like they were on fire, every step taken hurt the Staffie like nothing else he had ever experienced before. Also he was feeling noticably weaker.

As they marched on further into the darkness, Benson had started to get a scent. He could smell water. Dark dank and smelly water.

He realised they must be nearing the Black River.

Meowla, King, Old Joe and Bounce padded along behind. They were all surrounded by a good thirty Huufenuffs.

Bad tempered Huffenuffs at that!!

All they seemed to do, all the way was argue with each other.

Arimus of Huff led the way, walking next to Benson.

Arimus had actually been talking to Benson. Telling him ,mostly how strong and brave the Huffenuffs were.

One thing to remember dear reader is that Huffenuffs just love talking. Their favorite topic ,of course, was themselves. How brave and bold and fearless they were.

Benson had gathered from what Arimus was saying, that they were all, at one time as wolves. But the ancient ones had punished them, for following Ragnar. They had been banished to the fabled lands, sentenced to live in the dark caves and forests. Also some had been banished, with the wolves, in to the two legger world.

That made Benson think. He realised how old Earthly legends had been formed over the many centuries.

Things like, trolls, dwarfs, and were-wolves.

Horrors, just thought nowadays to be stories to frighten children. But of course it made sense, when you actually see a Huffenuff, you can understand how the myths evolved.

Huffenuffs were indeed fearsome looking creatures. Enough to give anyone nightmares.

Arimus was, of course very proud of this.

There was much pushing and shoving, and more arguments, as the band of "Arimus,said Benson, we do need to rest a while".

Arimus looked at Benson with a sneer. "Can't keep up eh?"he replied.

"The great Benson The Dog. Emissary of The Mighty Protector,tired?

However,Arimus could not seem to help shivering, as he spoke the name of the great tree.

"We just need some time to rest,replied Benson. My friends and I have come far!".

Arimus begrudgingly agreed.

"He turned around and made a loud growling kind of shout.

"Huffenuffs hold up!!!..

Huffenuffs halted in their tracks.

"Let these creatures rest a while, sneered Arimus.

"In fact, he continued, we will spend the night here. Make up some fires, and cover.But watch these creatures carefully. We are due at the Black River by morning!!"

There was a hubub of voices, as the Huffenuffs left the five friends in a small group, and made their way into groups themselves. More than likely for more arguing and boasting.

"And keep the noise down!!!", raged Arimus.

With that the Huffenuffs got busy. Some collecting wood, and others fashioning crude cover with the available sticks and bracken.

Benson and his friends sat round in a small circle.

"This is it,my dear friends", Bernson whispered.

"You four, must make a break for it!"

"You must get away from here, and then track me, and the Huffenuffs to the Black River,. without being seen!!"

"Why can't we all get away?,queried King. We will not leave you here alone!!"

"King, dear King, said Benson sadly. This is why I was sent. This is what I, and I alone must do, but if you track us to the river, then you may be needed".

"I am not sure how, or quite why as yet?, but The Great Tree sent you with me, until we reach the Black River. Then I must cross alone!'

" Now, if you all can get away from these creatures, it may give us an edge?'

"The element of surprise?".

The four friends looked at each other. They were all filled with a great unease.

"Okay, said Benson, I think the best plan is this. I will cause a diversion, and when I do the rest of you scat!, away into the hills, and forest cover. King, old friend, I will need you to help me?".

"No problem!!, replied the great Alsation.

"You cause some mayhem, over where the Huffenuffs are making their camps. I will deal with Arimus!".

"The rest of you, as soon as they are distracted run away to cover, just as fast as you can!"

The friends nodded, so solemn was their demeanour.

"Right, said Benson. Here I go!"

Benson stood to his feet, and padded over to where Arimus sat.

"Arimus!, said Benson loudly. I don't believe you are as brave as you make out to be?".

"In fact, I know - for a fact - that you are a coward!!".

Arimus could not believe what he was hearing. He stood up in front of Benson, he was visiblely shaking with Huffenuff, gruff rage.

Benson squared up to Arimus. His feet apart and his big Staffie chest puffed out, as far as he could make it.

"Whoa!, warned Benson. Remember Arimus, Ragnar wants me alive?".

"Alive yes, sneered the creature, but he did not say in what condition!!".

But just before he could attack Benson, King made his move.

King leapt high in the air, landing dead centre- amidst the main group of bewildered Huffenuffs.

King landed in a crouch, his big shaggy head darting this way and that. Suddenly he let out a loud fearsome growl..The Huffenuffs seemed momentarily stunned to silence. But, for all their nastyness, they were in fact rather brave. Well they were actually too stupid to feel normal fear.

A group of them shouting, and brandishing little axes made a charge for King.

King smiled a large toothy grin, and threw himself at the approaching creatures. His massive paws and claws battering and disabling huffenuffs all over the place.He collected some in his jaws, and after giving them a good shaking, he sent the stunned creatures flying over his head, they landed in a huge pile of arms, legs and confusion.

As King battled away with the angry Huffenuffs, Meowla, Bounce and Old Joe Mole, scuttled away discreatly into the cover of the nearby bracken.

There they made their way up and over the small hillocks and safely into the woodlands.

Meanwhile, Arimus was shouting for attention. At the same time holding a sharp little axe to Benson's throat.

The Staffie was just sitting, quietly, on his haunches, watching the confused mayhem play out. He was ginning the Staffie grin as he did so.

King saw this, realising it was time for his departure, and with a howl and a growl he, bit, battered, and punched his way through the remaining Huffenuffs, off and away into the cover of the bracken covered hillside.

"Nice one King!",Benson thought. So proud of his fearless old friend.

Arimus turned to Benson.

"Stupid creature, stupid dog, he blustered, this will do you no good at all!"

"Keep your hair on!" teased Benson. "What's your problem anyway?,surely it's me that Ragnar wants?".

Arimus stamped his feet! Arimus cursed and swore. Arimus Huffed and gruffed. Suddenly striking Benson hard on the head with the handle of his axe!

Benson was stunned by the blow. He fell to the ground. As he fell, he felt darkness enveloping him.

Benson passed out...

Arimus not content with this, began kicking Benson's unconcious body in temper!

"Get a stretcher prepared", he growled. Bind him and twine him tightly.

"We will drag the wrethched dog to the Black River!!"

The dishevelled Huffenuffs obeyed their leader.

They found wood, rope and twine.

Building a sturdy stretcher, they roughly lay Benson's unconcious body on the top.

They bound and tied him securely. So tight, in fact were his bonds, that they cut deep into his fur and skin.

"RIGHT - HUFFENUFFS,- GET MOVING!!' bawled Arimus.

"We march to the Black River!!".

From the protective cover of the woodlands, King and the rest of the group had watched all this happen.

"They'll pay for that growled King. I swear by the Mighty Protector!"

"Whatever happens they will pay!!!".

"Come", yapped Bounce. "We must follow!".

They all re-grouped. Bounce leading with Meowla, and King, with Old Joe on his back walked behind. They could see which way the Huffenuffs travelled quite clearly from the rise of the woodland hill side.

The group followed carefully. They walked deep in thought.

It was just about that time when they were stopped in their tracks!!
It was then that they all heard it.
Even above the rage, and bluster of the great storms.
They clearly heard the howling.
That Blood curdling howl..
They did not have to be told from whom it came.
It could only have been Ragnar's howl.
The Howl of The Black Wolf.
 Unease and sadness plagued the close companions, as they resumed their journey.
Old Joe no longer sang!...

CHAPTER NINE.   The Last Stand.

Benson The Dog, slipped in and out of consciousness.
He could feel himself being dragged along on the make-shift stretcher.
Bumping and tipping over each obsacle. Every bump hurt the Staffie, very badly indeed.
He bonds were so tight they were cutting into his skin, and he felt bruised all over. He felt like he done ten rounds with a big boxer dog?
The thought almost made hime smile. Only that his jaw ached far too much for any smiling.
Always time for a bit of humour , he thought.
He could hear bits of conversation that went on between the Huffenuffs.
Well, that is if you could call it conversation?, All they ever seemed to do was argue about the stupidest of things.
But he could clearly hear Arimus of Huff, bawling orders, and threats at his band of cohorts.
He heard Arimus shout , that they were nearing the Black River. Actually he didn't need to hear that piece of news, because he could clearly smell it!
It was an awful smell.

You know when perhaps, you may have found a dead rabbit or animal in your garden? Well it smelt rather like, that but far worse! Dreadful and dank!

The smell grew steadily worse until..

"Right you Huffenuffs!!, bawled Arimus, here we are, this is close enough for any Huffenuff!!"

"Untie th dog!!"

"But leave on the muzzle!"

When they had tied Benson down on to the stretcher, they had muzzled him as well. As a final indignation.

Benson could feel his bonds being loosened. What a blessed relief, he thought.

Once the Huffenuffs had finished getting rid of the rope and twine, they unceremoniously, rolled Benson of the stretcher, leaving him in a heap on the ground.

Benson slowly opened his eyes. He did not want any of the Huffenuffs to notice that he had awoken.

He squinted, carefully looking around. Trying hard, to get an idea of where he was, and the lay of the land.

He could see the Huffenuffs in little groups, they seemed to be setting up camp.

Sure enough! He then heard Arimus shout!

"Come on get to it!! Build a decent camp. We will have to stay here over night at least!!".

Arimus of Huff continued..

"We aint crossing The Black River. The Great Black Wolf has forbidden us to cross!, well at least for now!".

"The dog has to cross on his own?".

"Once the camp is built, nice and solid, and a guard has been set up, then we can get him ready to go"

"Because remember, his wretched mates escaped?..thanks to you lot!!".

"So we don't want any trouble from them?".

"Now dooo weee!!". He finished the last sentence, half shout, but mostly growling!.

Benson watched as the Huffenuffs leapt into action.
Running about, like chickens with no heads! No kind of
system involved there thern, Benson mused.
As he watched Benson could see them,some gathering
wood, and others rope and twine, and others, that just
seem spend time tripping over the rest?
All huffy and gruffy and arguing. Each Huffenuff,
blaming the other.
While all this confusion continued,Benson waited, and
watched.

The Happiness Tree stood alone.
The darkness had covered all of Sleepy Dog Land.
He felt sick and weak, and so very - very sad.
There was a glimpse of the Sleepy Dog Land moon
overhead.
But not as he had ever seen it.
Instead of the large , bright and jolly globe.
The moon was pale and white. Hardly giving off any
moon light whatsoever.
Everything was different. The shadows seemed longer,
and almost menacing.
Then he knew, in fact - he was not alone.
Nearby was a large, and very long dark shadow.
Darker than all the rest.
The Happiness Tree spoke.
"So you've come!".
"Speak wolf!"
"I know you are here!!, I have been expecting you!!".
The shadow moved.
Seemed to lengthen as it stood.
"So,oh great tree, you knew I would come?",sneered
Ragnar.
"Yes I have come, come to speak to my vanquished
foe!!".
"You are ahead of yourself Ragnar!",replied the
Happiness Tree.

"I am far from vanquished!", the old magic will be played out. Played out as it has been written!!".
Ragnar growled at this!
"You must know I am more powerful than you, or any of your doggy children!!"
"I am the ancient magic!!". I am so much older than you!!".
I have awoken. I walk these lands, as and where I want!. The darkness follows me!"
"You send a CHILD!, TO FACE ME?" Ragnar howled and the storms raged.
Ragnar walked closer to the tree in menacing fashion. But still keeping a good distance between himself and the tree.
"Come closer Black Wolf", taunted the Happiness Tree. "Why do you not come closer and talk with me?"
Ragnar sneered, a toothy sneer at the tree.
"We really do not have anything to talk about, now do we?".
"Ragnar,continued the Happiness Tree, we can work this out?.
Why fight, why bring all down with us?". "You were once a soldier, a general!!"
"You led followers, you ruled these lands!".
Ragnar remained silent, as he slowly walked closer to the tree. His red eyes glowing bright like fire.
"They cheated me, he growled. They took from me my very essence, and made you!!".Made you..!!".
Ragnar, threw his head back and howled,showing the gap where his fang had been.
"They punished me, they banished me to the fabled lands!, sending my followers away also. To populate that worthless two legger world , as you call it!. Those two leggers breeding my people into submission. Their true natures lost forever. In a mix of "dog breeds!!!".

"But now I am back!", continued Ragnar. I walk once
more. I will take back what is mine by right!!".
"Go now Ragnar!", The Happiness Tree replied. "Go
now from whence you came!".
The old magic will decide!".
"The Higher Power, will choose right from wrong!".
"The End Game, must be played!"
As he finished his words, the Great Tree raised his
boughs, began to grow!
A green and pulsating glow surrounded the mighty
protector. Casting beams of the magical light on to
Ragnar himself.
"Go now!! Black Wolf!, go now and face your destiny.
As we all must do!"
With that The Black Wolf moved back, quickly, from
the tree. The geen light seemed to singe his fur.
He yelped like a whipped dog. For a moment, losing all
his great, and terrifying statuer.
There was peels of thunder from the sky.
Then he was gone.!
The Happiness Tree, feeling so very weary, sank back
down into himself.
The bright green light slowly faded.
All was quiet, all was dark..

Night was drawing in fast back in the Two Legger
World.
Although, really and truly, one couldn't tell the
difference between daylight and night time. The storms
were still very bad indeed, and growing worse.
The news reports were often, and many. Obviously the
media loved what was going on. They just loved making
everything seem worse than it actually was.
But this time they really didn't need to exagerate things.
It really was that bad.
They were getting reports of vast amounts of trees,
being pulled up, and destroyed, by the strong gale force
winds.

All over the world it was happening. Here in England, the great Forest Of Dean, an ancint woodland, had been almost descimated. The local forsetry commison, were in turmoil.

Not just trees being pulled up by the storms. But trees that were just withering and dying before their eyes. This was unheard of, up until now!.

Jack and Sheila were still in the den with Benson. Mum had just brought them sandwiches and milk.

"Come on you two, she soothed, you have to eat! "You won't be able to help Benson by making yourselves ill?".

She left the plate of sandwiches, and glasses of milk with the children.

"She's right, said Jack.

"We are going to need our strength and courage tonight!".

"Remember what The Happiness Tree said to us before!".

"Benson is going to need us!"

Sheila agreed, and they both tucked in to the food hungrily.

All the time Jack kept the warm, and faintly glowing wooden key, in his hand.

As if he was afraid to let it go.

"Midnight", said Jack thoughtfully.

"Midnight is the time we can at least help Benson!!".

"Help Benson and everything else?,Sheila asked.

"Yeah Sis, that about sums it up..!!".

They sat and watched the sky, as it turned from black to inky blue as the storms blustered and raged.

King and the gang, were in a reasonable position to see what was happening,on the banks of the Black River. They had watched as Benson had been untied, and left motionless on the black muddy river side. They had seen the Huuffenuffs building and constructing their camp.

King had noticed straight away, that the Huffenuffs had placed guards around the camp site.

"That's clever, he growled. Almost too clever for Huffenuffs?",he continued.

"We must not under estimate the Huffenuffs, warned Meowla. They may be gruff, rude and stupid in a lot of ways. But we must be careful, and very wary of them!!".

"Agreed, said King.

"But we must think of some way to rescue Benson!".

"But what of the old words?", queried Meowla.

"Aye, interupted Old Joe Mole, Them there ancient words say, he moost goo oover th' river by himself?".

"Soo they doo!!".

"Let's try and remember them," woofed Bounce...

"King sat on his haunches and recited the ancient words in full..

So the ancient ones say
night may soon conquer day
though our Mighty Protector still stands.
But as time passes by
he might wither and die
and the darkness will cover our land.
Then a hero must rise
blazing truth fills his eyes
with pure goodness and strength in his heart.
With a quest he must make
there's a journey to take
so Sleepy Dog Land will not fall apart.

To Ragnar's Tooth he must go
a fabled land deep below
where the black river flows to the sea.
Sacrifice must be made
for the treasure he"ll trade
granting life to The Happiness Tree.
If the tree once more stands
dark must flee from our land

as the roots of protection re-form.
Once the magic's bestowed
to satisfy ancient codes
only then Sleepy Dog Land's re-born.

"There, said King. The ancient words are spoken!".
You see, Benson must go alone,and of his own free
will!".
"That is part of Ragnar's plan!"
"That is why the Huffenuffs were told to capture us?"
"So that they will send Benson across the Black River.
Then, you see, he will not have crossed of his own
accord, he was made to cross?".
So that would go against the ancient magic?"
They all agreed.
"What doo we dooo eh?", asked Old Joe.
"Yes, and what did the Great Tree mean about, using all
of our talents?", questioned Bounce.
"I haven't got any talents?, well not a special one?".
"Our talents will come when needed", said King.
"We must, in the meantime, get Benson free!", time is
short, and The Black Wolf close!".
King, peered out of the bracken, and continued
watching what was happening.
All seemed quiet. The Huffenuffs were all encamped.
Benson was laying a little way off from the creatures.
"They even have Benson muzzled??, growled King.
"Those creatures have Benson muzzled!!"
"Now is the time!!". King stood up, shook himself
vigerously.
King continued.
"You must all follow my lead, he whispered. I will
make my move, you will all follow when safe".
"I am going to get Benson away from those creatures,
whatever it takes!".
"I want the rest of you to get across the Black River the
best way you can?".

"With luck, the Huffenuffs will have enough to contend with when I make my entrance. So you three can get further down the river bank, and some how cross.!".
"No matter what the ancient words say, Benson is going to need us, more than ever!!
"But we must not cross until we see that Benson is across safely. On his own!!".
King gave a long look, at each of his friends in turn. They nodded back at King.
"Just have faith", finished the big German Sheppard.
"Just have faith in yourselves and The Mighty Protector!!".
With that king stood on all fours, and crouched low! His chestnut fur stood on end, right down his long ,strong back.
The he sprang up, and out of the bracken's cover.
King ran headlong at the groups of Huffenuffs, barking and snarling wildly.
He must have made for a fearsome sight!
Suddenly there was a call of alarm in the Huffenuff camp.
They had seen the huge, growling, snarling and woofing Alsation, coming full belt towards them!
Now, as we know the Huffenuffs are brave, but the sight of King, racing down the rocky bank towards them, must have unnerved the bravest, or the stupidest Huffenuff.
As king was running, all guns blazing, he caught sight of Benson trying to get to his feet.
Hold on old friend, thought King, I'm coming - I'm coming!!!
In seconds King was in the middle of the shocked Huffenuffs.
Bashing, and throwing with his paws, slashing and cutting, with his huge claws!!
Biting and chewing with his great teeth! King was awesome in battle.

He faught his way through groups of startled Huffenuffs, until he reached where Benson was now standing.

Their eyes met. King gave Benson a knowing glance. "Get going Benson, panted King, I will keep these lot busy, get going - away Benson!!" King gave Benson a grin, at the same time he passed a sharp claw over the twine that was holding on Benson's muzzle around his mouth.

The muzzle fell to the ground, Benson woofed at King with thanks.

King winked, and turned back into the battles fray.

King was so brave, thought Benson, as he made his way along the river bank towards some rock cover. A loyal and brave friend indeed. He could hear Kings growls and barks. Also he could hear Huffenuffs screaming, and shouting. Loudest of all, he could hear Arimus Of Huff's voice.

"Get him, get that wretched dog".

Just as Benson reached the rocky cover, he turned to see King, at last over powered by sheer numbers of angry Huffenuffs.

He watched as King went down under a pile of the vile creatures. He saw the glint of Arimus axe. Suddenly there was a loud howl and whine. Then silence.He hid himself behind the rock cover and watched as the groups of Huffenuffs, still left standing, moved away, leaving the proud and brave German Sheppard laying in a heap on the muddy river bank. Benson could see that King was badly wounded. He was laying so still.

Benson watched,in great sadness, and mounting anger, as the Huffenuffs started to drag Kings body towards the Black River. They huffed and puffed as they pulled the great dog through the mud.

Once they reached the waters edge, Benson watched in dismay as they pushed and rolled King into the rivers dark waters.

Benson watched as King floated for a moment and then just seemed to sink beneath the dark, dank water.
"One down for Ragnar",cried Arimus Of Huff.
"Now go and find the Stafford dog.!!".
"He must be found!".
Benson took stock of his surroundings.
I have to get across, he thought. But how?
The river was wide, and very deep. The smell of it was making him sick to his stomach.
But he must cross..
So Benson eased himself into the murky river.
Using his best 'doggy paddle', Benson started to swim.
Started to slowly swim, towards the distant shore.

While all this had been going on, Bounce, Old Joe and Meowla had been moving slowly through the cover of bracken and rocks. They had made their way around the Huffenuff camp. Now all they had to do was reach the rocky caves and caverns, on the bank of the Black River, without being seen.
This they managed to do. Well, the Huffenuffs were in total chaos, after Kings attack. They had little time to notice the three friends, manoeuvring around them to safety.
There were little groups of them arueing, about whom had the most painful wounds, or whom had put up a better fight. They were frantically running about in circles looking for Benson.
The three friends had seen all that happened. They had seen King valiently fighting, and they had seen him fall. Old Joe was inconsolable.
He, and King, after a rocky start, had built up a true, and strong friendship, over the long journey from Sleepy Dog Land.
The three sat in the small rocky cavern, trying plan their next move.
"Benson got away, purred Meowla. I saw him start swimming across the river.!".

"But King is dead!!'...Old Joe was beside himself!.".
Bounce and Meowla tried to comfort Joe.
"He knew all the time..sobbed Old Joe, he knew they
would kill him?".
"He did what he had to do, woofed Bounce, he did what
he knew to be right!!".
"Won't bring him back though..will it?",sobbed Joe.
"Just remember what King told us Joe, soothed Meowla,
"We have to have faith!".
"We have to be strong!!".
"Yes, said Bounce, and we have to get over the Black
River!!".
"Yes, we dooo, replied Old Joe, and I know how!

CHAPTER TEN   The End Game Is Played.

Benson reached the far bank of the Black River.
Coughing and sputtering, he pulled himself out of the
water, and on to the muddy bank.
He lay for a moment panting and coughing.
Then raised himself up, on to his feet. He stood, and
vigerously shook as much of the dirty water out of his
fur as possible.
Benson stood looking out at the fabled lands, known as
Ragnar's Tooth.
He thought, well I've made it this far.
Just then he heard a long and searching howl. He stood
stock still!
He couldn't move?
The howl rang out loudly in his ears, and seemed to run
through his whole body. Snout to tail. He suddenly
knew for certain.
The Black Wolf, he thought. He knows I am here!
"Yes, oh Benson The Dog. Benson the emissary. I know
you are here!".
"In fact - I welcome you!"
Ragnar's voice growled in Benson's head."

"Look ahead, continued the voice. Look ahead and I will lead you to me!".
"I would talk with you!".
Benson shivered.
"Oh Mighty Protector, be with me, walk with me?",
Benson spoke these words out loud.
"Aaaahhh, you seek comfort from the tree?, sneered the voice. You expect the tree to help you?".
"Your Great Tree, your Mighty Protector, he withers! He is near death as we speak!".
"Now, look you ahead!..Follow the trail towards the black mountain caverns.
There I will meet with you!". The voice sneered and growled.
"There, you will come face to face with your fate..!!".
Benson said nothing for a moment.
Then he spoke, out loud.
"I will come to you Ragnar!".
"For it is my destiny!".
The voice just laughed and teased in Benson's mind.
Benson shook himself, and started walking, towards the caves, darkly yawning in the mountain's side.

Bounce and Meowla, sat quietly. Listening to Old Joe's plan.
"That's it, eeh by goom!".
"That's how we'll dooo it!".
"We will go under the river!!".
Meowla and Bounce looked at each other, and then back at Joe.
"Underneath the river?.queried Meowla.
"How ar we going to do that?".
"Well, I'm a mole?. Granted, I am a dog and a mole!".
Bounce, could'nt help giggling at this!
"Sssshhh Bounce", scolded Meowla, let him finish.
Bounce nodded, and sat back on his haunches listening.
Old Joe Mople, continued.

"Well being a doggy, and a mole, he said, what is it we are best at?"
Bounce looked at Meowla and she at him.
"Digging!, Joe exclaimed. Digging and tunneling!".
"I will tunnel down into this soft black ground.
"Now, behind me will be Bounce. He is bigger than me, so he will tunnel from my digging, making the tunnel big enough for Meowla to follow. Being a cat she can't tunnel?".
"It's the only way!", concluded Old Joe.
Bounce and Meowla, reluctantly agreed to Joe's plan.
"Reet then thou knows!!", chirped Joe.
"Here we go"!!.
With that Joe started burrowing into the soft muddy ground.
Soil flying away from his little feet at an extreemly rapid pace.
Soon he had disappeared into the ground, and Bounce started digging in behind him.
Progress was good. As Bounce disappeared into the tunnel behind Joe, Meowla followed. Trying to keep her eyes and mouth shut, for fear of a mouthful of soil.
Joe dug downwards for a while, until he instinctively knew when they had reached below the water line. Then he was burrowing ahead at a fantastic rate.
Bounce had a really hard job just keeping up with him.
With Meowla following, our three friends finally reached the far bank of the Black River.
Joe came up first. Carefully checking that there was no one about to spot their arrival.
Bounced followed him, with Meowla coming above ground last.
Meowla immediately started cleaning off the mud and dirt from her fur, as the Mole-Dog and Bounce shook themselves clean.
"Told ya!!".exclaimed Joe proudly.
"Yes you did indeed!", soothed Meowla.

"Yes, well done Joe", praised Bounce.

"I sense Benson, said Bounce. He is travelling towards those mountain caverns.

"Here, follow me you two, I will snout out his trail".

Meowla and Joe waited while Bounce sniffed and snouted.

Until suddenly, Bounce pricked up his ears, and pawed the ground.

"I've got it, he said, I've got Benson's scent".

"Follow me!".

The other two did as Bounce asked, and followed.

The three friends headed, silently towards the Mountains.

Meanwhile, back on Two Legger world, it was not far off the midnight hour.

Jack and Sheila were alone with Benson in the den.

Sheila had Benson's head in her lap, and was gently stroking his ears.

"Remember how much he liked haviung his ears stroked?" ,said Sheila ,with sadness in her voice.

"Now come on Sis, replied Jack, don't think like that!"

"All may yet be well?".

"Yes, said Sheila, we just have to be strong and have faith!!".

"But it's so difficult!".

The storms were shouting and screaming outside the window!.

"Look at the time Sis?", said Jack. Soon it will be time!".

He felt the wooden key in his hand, it was pulsing with a quiet, green and warm energy.

"I had better get ready!"

Jack got up off the sofa and went into his bedroom. He came back out dressed his big blue anorak and beany hat.

The clock on the wall read 11.50pm.

Jack spoke.

"Right then Sis, now you are to stay here with Benson.
Hold him tight, and keep him comfy!".
I will go downstairs and into the garden!".
Remember if Mum or Dad comes in, just try and make
an excuse for me?
"They won't understand what needs to be done!".
"Okay Jack, replied his sister, I will do my best. But
please be careful!!".
Jack smiled and nodded at his sister, and left the den.
Very quietly closing the door.

Benson The Dog had, at last reached the mountain
caverns.
He came to a halt just outside, what seemed to be the
largest and darkest cave of all.
Just above the ceiling of rock , Benson could see the
pale moon. It looked massive from where he was
standing. But it gave no real light to speak of.
Just like a big, two legger style paper plate, he thought.
The storms and gales were blowing and blustering. The
rain felt like little needles pricking his skin.
As Benson looked above the rocks at the moon, a
strange and large shadow seemed to appear and grow in
front of his eyes?
The shadow began to take shape, against the pale moon.
All of a sudden it took shape. Benson could see the
outline of darkness had now become wolf!. Black
Wolf!.
Indeed it was Ragnar!.
His silhouette stood large, and looked fearsome.
Benson watched, with mounting unease, as the Ragnar
shadow threw back his head and howled.
Against the moon - Ragnar looked a terrible sight
indeed!

The howling finished. Ragnar looked down from the
rocks, and straight at Benson The Dog.

His deep red eyes seeming to burn into Benson's very soul.

"So, whispered The Black Wolf, you have come!".

With that Ragnar leapt off the rock, and down, landing in front of a startled Benson.

"I-Iam here", Benson stammered.

"You really are a fool, sneered Ragnar. A brave fool though?, I'll give you that Benson!".

"Brave, doesn't come into this Ragnar, I am just doing what I have to do!".

"Come with me Benson The Dog!, you must follow me!".

Benson nodded.

Ragnar turned and led Benson into the mouth of the dark cavern.

Inside the cavern, seemed just the same as outside, weather wise anyway.

It was huge. Easily the size of a two legger football pitch.

Even though they were now inside the cave, the wind and rain was still beating down.

There were rock shelves running round the cave walls. Rocks hanging from the roof in various shapes.

In the centre of the cave, stood a huge table shaped rock.

To the right of the great rock table was a pit. From the pit came the noise, and bluster of the storms. Benson looked but could not see down, as all was deep blackness. Though, there did seem to be a faintish, blue glow coming from where ever the bottom of the pit was?

This was not a pit, thought Benson. This was an abyss.

Ragnar jumped, and landed in the centre of the table rock. Turning round to Benson, the Black Wolf sat on his haunches.

Benson could only stare, in a kind of scary admiration, for the huge creature.

Ragnar was indeed huge. It made Benson understand what it must have been like for Old Joe Mole, standing next to the brave King.

The fur of the Black Wolf was ragged and shaggy. Pitch black in colour. So black that it didn't seem like fur at all, but a sort of deep darkness with no ending.

Ragnar's face was huge as well. In fact the more Benson looked into those burning red eyes, the larger the face became?

Almost hypnotic.

Ragnar grinned, a wide wolf grin, at Benson.

Benson could easily see the fangs of the great wolf. Large and sharp.

Benson suddenly noticed. There were only three front fangs.

Two at the top, and one at the bottom. The right hand lower fang was missing.

"I have come for your other tooth Ragnar", Benson heard himself saying.

"I will have it!!".

"I must have it!".

Ragnar looked at Benson. His stare was one of shock?

"You would dare say that to me, ME!!", Ragnar spluttered.

"I could kill you right now?, yet you DARE say that to me??"

.Benson said nothing in reply. The Staffie just sat back on his haunches, all the time looking at Ragnar.

Ragnar, leapt off the rock, and landed lightly in front of Benson.

Now while this confrontation was going on, neither Ragnar or Benson had noticed the three smaller shadows that had entered the cavern.

Meowla, Bounce and Old Joe, silently crept into the cave.

They could see Ragnar and Benson clearly, and they listened to all that was being said.

"How can we help?,whispered Bounce.
"Ssssh Bounce, said Meowla quietly. We must wait and watch. We will know what to do?", some how we will know!"..
"Wait, interupted Joe, look what is happening.
They all watched.
"I WILL have your tooth Ragnar, growled Benson.
Lives and worlds depend on it.!!!".
Suddenly Ragnar made a swing, at Benson with his huge paw.
The blow caught Benson full in the snout! The sharp claws cut into Benson's nose.
The blow sent the Staffie flying back against the wall of rock. Benson was badly winded. He panted and tried hard to get to his feet, but his legs felt as weak as water.
Ragnar leapt again at Benson. The Black Wolf landed, his legs astride Benson The Dog. Benson felt sick and weak. His vision was blurred. He could feel, and smell Ragnars dank breath on his face.
Benson tried to wriggle free, but the huge paws of the wolf held him fast.
Benson looked from the side of his eyes, He was backed up against the cavern wall, to one side, and on the other loomed the dreadful pit. The bottomless abyss.
There was no escape.
Ragnar stood over Benson, panting, and growling fiercly.
Suddenly all Benson could think about was the Happiness Tree.
In his mind he started to recite the ancient words:

Hail 'The Happiness Tree'
In a place we all go.
With a wagging of tail
and a bright shiny nose.
Greet The Happiness Tree
he's so ancient and wise
such wisdom and truth

he will know if we've lied.
Praise the Happiness Tree
always gentle and kind
as he dries all those tears
that our lives leave behind.
He has lived here forever
see how proudly he stands
mighty wooded protector
watching over our land...
Awaken great tree
Awaken for our sakes..

Ragnar could hear Benson. He could hear Benson's thoughts, so strong was the Staffies resolve and faith.
As Benson completed the prayer, Ragnar looked, and felt visibly shaken.
He stood back from Benson, growling and howling, all at the same time.
But more shocks were in store for the Black Wolf.
As Ragnar stared at Benson, the Staffie began looking rather different.
Now surrounding them both was a deep green light.
The light seemed to come from Benson's body itself.
Ragnar tried desperately to jump, and pull himself back from the warm green glow.
But to no avail. He seemed stuck fast!
Whilst all the time, Benson's body seemed to grow, and change.
His fur seemed some how wooden. Foliage seemed to grow and wave from his body, like branches and boughs.
Ragnar was, for a moment frozen to the spot.
Benson realised that now was the time for action . He wasn't certain what kind of action he was going to take?
But suddenly, something inside him had decided what to do.
Benson moved fast and acurately, almost like a striking snake.

He bared his teeth, and shot a bite at Ragnars jaw!

The wolf tried to pull back, but the green light held him fast.

He howled, and screamed in pain, as he felt Benson's teeth, surround and clamp on to his remaining bottom fang.

Benson twisted and pulled.

He felt Ragnar's remaining fang come away into his mouth.

"Now hissed Meowla, my time is now!!"..

With that she flew off the shelf of rock, and landed with natural Cat agility, on to the rock table behind Ragnar and Benson.

Ragnar was howling, growling, and stamping his great paws. He was in the most terrible of tempers.

Benson, half laying, and half sitting, panting and whimpering in pain.

The long, sharp fang fell out of Benson's mouth, rolling in between the two dogs.

Ragnar saw it, and made a lung for his precious tooth.

But quick as you like, there was a blur of white and ginger fur, as Meowla The Cat Queen, flew off the rock table and picked up the tooth with her mouth.

This was not easy, as the tooth was very large, and her mouth very small.

But she managed.

Ragnar barked and growled, and flew at Meowla. But Benson had managed to raise himself, and he moved his aching body, in between Ragnar and Meowla.

As Ragnar lunged at the cat. But Benson managed to get his mouth around Ragnar's left leg. Benson bit in deep, and held on,with a terriers grip. He held on for dear life.

He looked at Meowla. The cat seemed to understand without words. She nodded to Benson, and still holding the precious tooth jumped up, and over the rocks. Back to the high shelf where the others were hiding.

They all watched, as the Black Wolf, and Benson fought for their lives.

Ragnar was clawing, and pawing, and biteing Benson without mercy.

The noise was terrible.

Ragnar had Benson backed up against the cave wall.

Just then , as Benson thought all was lost. Ragnar stopped.

He spoke holding Benson fast as he did so.

"I will get that tooth back, sneered Ragnar. "Know that I will Benson. And know all this you have done? All a waste of time.!!

He howled loud and long, and then suddenly he bared his teeth, ready to make the death bite to Benson's exposed throat.

All the time Benson had been waiting. He had managed to get the tooth and hold Ragnar at bay.

Now was his time..!!

Now was his destiny!!!.

So before the Black Wolf could strike, Benson made his move.

He shot his mouth at Ragnar's shoulder. He felt his teeth make contact and he bit in hard!!

At the same time he wrapped his arms around the Black Wolf's neck.

Ragnar seemed stunned. He just stared in disbelief as Benson pulled and rolled him self over. The two fell together, landing on the edge of the dark pit of the abyss.

Benson released his teeth from the wolf's shoulder.

Benson sighed, and shouted". "For you oh Mighty Protector.

"I do this for you..!!!! "...

The words spoken, Benson pulled, and rolled. Using every ounce of strength he had left.

All of a sudden Ragnar seemed to know what was happening. He stared at Benson in that split second, with an expression of anger and disbelief.

Benson smiled back at Ragnar.

Benson aimed all his weight and pushed.

Then they both fell.

Ragnar's last words were a howl of sudden realisation, and fear.

They toppled and fell into the bottomless abyss.

The three friends watched in disbelief.

They watched as Ragnar and Benson disappeared into the pit.

As they did so, the warm green light seemed to get brighter and brighter.

The winds howled, and the rains became torrents of rushing water.

Then came the lightening.

From deep inside the pit, lightening bolts exploded into the dark cave. The cavern was bright with electric power.

At the very same time the lightening would strike the Happiness Tree.

The Great Tree had watched all that had taken place. He knew what was to happen next. He mused with a great sadness. Benson has made the ultimate sacrifice. The ancient magic must soon be appeased.

As these thoughts rushed through the mind of the Happiness Tree, the lightening struck the Great Tree at his top most bough. Splitting The Mighty Protector completely in two. Leaving The Mighty Protector in smokey ruins.

Jack had planted the key, deep into the roots of the Yew Tree. As the Happiness Tree had told him.

He had done this at the exact same time that the bright and powerful lightening bolts had struck the small tree.

The Yew Tree had shuddered and lit up so brightly, Jack had thought it might explode.

The bolts of forked lightening had struck the tree at the trunk. The tree had groaned and then just slipped over to one side. It's branches and trunks smoldering and smoking.

Jack had been thrown clear back across the garden by the impact of the lightening.

But he had managed to pick himself up, and get back inside the house, before anyone saw him.

Jack quietly clambered up the stairs and back into the warm den with his sister."It's done Sis, said Jack. It's done!".

"Oh Jack, cried Sheila.."What is it Sis?..

"It's Benson Jack, I- I don't think he's breathing?, sobbed Sheila.

"I think Benson has died?"...

Jack rushed over to the sofa.

Sure enough, Benson was laying silently, and very still indeed...

Bounce, Meowla and Old Joe, padded, pawed and scurried out of the smoke filled cavern.

Meowla, still holding on to the tooth of Ragnar, safely in her small paw.

They pawed, padded, and scurried, well away from the hateful mountain cavern, until they reached the safety of the covered bracked foliage, that covered the smaller hillsides.

"Oh, byThe Great Tree", exclaimed Bounce The Westie.

"Benson The Dog, dead?...IT CAN'T BE SO?, Bounce woofed out the words between tears.

"But we all saw what happened", said Old Joe.

Meowla spoke. "I was close by Benson, she said, I saw exactly what happened".

"Benson pulled Ragnar's tooth, and I ,because of my great cat agility, managed to collect up the tooth in my mouth. As I did so Benson spoke to me!"

"Not in words, you understand. But his voice seemed to be in my head".

"He said we must get the tooth back, as quickly as possible to the Happiness Tree.Where you, Bounce and Old Joe must bury it deep within the roots of the Great Tree.

"This must be done before sun rise?".

"How do we get back so quickly?, queried Bounce. It's a good two days march back to the woodlands of The Mighty Protector?".

"Benson said we would have help, continued Meowla? But from where? They all looked around for any sign of help.

"Nothing, remarked Old Joe, Eeh by goom, there's nought about!'

"Well we must start back anyway, said Bounce. We must try our best to run back?"..

The animals turned towards the Black River, and began to head back. They crawled back through the underground tunnel, Joe and Bounce had made.

Out on to the river bank, near the Huffenuff encampment.

As they crawled out they noticed how very quite it was. In all the excitement, they had not realised that, in fact the great storms seemed to have ceased completely.

All was deathly quiet.

"We must be careful here, whispered Bounce. The Huffenuffs will be looking for us?".

"No they won't!!", came a voice. A familiar voice.

The three friends turned in panic to where the voice had come from.

There was King?!.

He was laying down and licking his legs and paws. There were cuts and bruises all over his chestnut coloured body. But he was alive!!

"King, oh King! me old mate ,eeeh it's good to see thee!! Old Joe was almost singing the words!!

"But we saw thee drown?"

"I am not certain, how, why or where? replied the Alsation.

I remember going down under the Huffenuffs, and I remember feeling the dark waters surround me. Then nothing.

Until I came to, awoke in a haze of green light. And suddenly, here I was? Alone, laying here, on the bank of the Black River.

"But I remember, well, I must have been dreaming. But I remember Benson standing there, he next to me as I was beginning to awaken".

"He told me, you three had the tooth of the Black Wolf, and that you would need my help, getting it back to Sleepy Dog Land".

"Then as I became fully awake, Benson was gone?".

"Where is he?, asked the Alsation, where is Benson?".

The three told King about all that had gone on in the dark cavern.

"The storms have ceased, said King. "Now we must get back!".

"But how?, queried Meowla.

"On my back!!", exclaimed King.

"Come on , all of you, up on my back!!".

The three friends looked at each other uneasily. But did as they were told.

Meowla climbed up first, followed by Old Joe, and Bounce ran and jumped and landed between the two.

"Ah - ha! shouted the great German Sheppard, the magic returns..

He suddenly seemed to get bigger, and bigger, and much bigger! Until it felt, for his passengers, like being aboard a small pony.

They all held on for dear life, as with a howl and woof, King started running, and running, and running, until he made one huge high leap, and proceeded to fly like a great eagle.

"Wahoooo - eeeh - oooh, aye oop, chimed Old Joe.

They soared above the dark and fabled lands, The Black River far down below now.

They could even see the band of Huffenuffs, running madly about, still in great confusion, and still deep in arguements, it seems.

But then again, it's no surprise really, as Huffenuffs will never change.

Because Huffenuffs, are simply, just Huffenuffs..

The great dog King howled, and his three friends cheered, as they flew faster, and faster, and higher and higher, until they were flying faster and higher, than had ever seemed possible. Heading towards Sleepy Dog Land, and the Happiness Tree.

Jack and Sheila were beside themselves.

Sheila in floods of tears, and Jack holding back his tears, with great difficulty.

They had called Mum and Dad.

"Oh kids, said Mum sadly. I am so very sorry, but it doesn't look good.

Benson does not seem to be breathing at all now?".

"But Dad has called the vet. He'll be hear very soon now!".

But what can he do?, asked Jack. I mean if Benson isn't breathing?".

"Let's wait and see, replied Mum. No point in thinking the worst!".

The time was around 3am, in Two Legger world.

Dad appeared round the den door, saying..."Mr.Moneygrabber, is on his way kids!".

"Now, in the meantime, get that big blanket from the airing cupboard, and wrap Benson in it. We must, at the very least, make sure he is comfy, whilst we wait for the vet. Jack obeyed, and brought the rug into the den, carefully covering Benson The Dog.

"And look the storms have died down, continued Dad. The moon is back!".

They all went to the window and looked out.

What a difference they saw.

All was quiet, and the sky was clear enough to see all the millions of twinkling stars. Everywhere seemed calm, and daylight bright, under the shinning moon.

Bounce, Old Joe Mole (The Dog) and Meowla, aboard the flying King, were just reaching the praire meadows of Sleepy Dog Land.

They could see the woodlands, beckoning them, clearly now.

"Nearly there shouted and woofted King. Hold tight, friends, hold tight now!!".

All three obeyed, and held clumps of the great dogs shaggy coat tightly in their paws.

King dipped down fast, towards the largest area of woodland. Which was home to their Mighty Protector.

All of a sudden, they were down. All three, rolling off Kings back, and on to the soft, leaf scattered soil of Sleepy Dog Land.

They all stood, some shaking, and some brushing the soil and leaves from their coats.

They stood and looked around.

"This is the correct woodland, said King. I recognise it. The Mighty Protector should be here?".

"Oh look hissed Meowla.

The turned to the direction of the cat's gaze.

Then they saw!

Where the Happiness Tree once stood, there was a pile of dead, and charred wood.

"Oh, are we too late?, cried Bounce.

"Has it all been for nothing?".

"Bury the tooth, urged Meowla. Like Benson said we should!".

"Just bury the tooth, it's all we can do?".

She padded over to the ruins of the tree, and dropped the tooth, from her mouth on to the soft wet soil.

"Dig Old Joe, dig!, and I'll dig behind you!', said Bounce sadly.'

Old Joe scurried over to where the cat was standing.
"Off I goes then!",said Joe.
"This is for thee, ooh mighty tree!!".
With that, Joe picked up the tooth, between his teeth,
and proceeded to burrow hard and fast! Hard and fast,
fast and hard, burrowed the small
Mole - Dog. Bounce took up the rear, and dug down,
behind Old Joe.
King and Meolwa watched and waited. There was wet
soil flying everywhere.
Then there was a period of quiet. Until Bounce and Old
Joe, suddenly came tumbling back, out of the small
tunnel.
"It be planted, sang Old Joe, OOH ya know, it be
planted!!".
The four friends, King, Meolwa, Bounce, and Old Joe
Mole, sat in a semi-circle around the tree ruins, and
waited.
Not at all sure what they waited for?, or what they
thought may happen.
They just sat, in silence, and quiet contemplation, and
waited.
It seemed like hours had gone by.
King broke the silence by saying..
"I think we should recite the ancient words?".
"I think we MUST recite the ancient prayer!".

The four animals all agreed, that this was what they
must do..
And this they did...
They all stood tall and they shouted, woofed, purred and
sqeaked out the ancient words - boldly and loudly - at a
star filled sky!!...

Hail 'The Happiness Tree'
In a place we all go.
With a wagging of tail
and a bright shiny nose.

Greet The Happiness Tree
he's so ancient and wise
such wisdom and truth
he will know if we've lied.
Praise the Happiness Tree
always gentle and kind
as he dries all those tears
that our lives leave behind.
He has lived here forever
see how proudly he stands
mighty wooded protector
watching over our land...
Awaken great tree
Awaken for our sakes..

The friends stood back.
They said nothing, they just waited, patiently and quietly, praying to their dear Happiness Tree.

Benson The Dog could feel himself falling.
Further and further down, down, down.
Or was he falling down?
Benson was not certain about this? All he knew is that he had taken hold of Ragnar and pulled them both, into the dark pit. They had been falling together.
At least he thought they had been?
But now it was just him, just Benson The Dog, falling, faster and faster.
He knew he must be travelling some where?
But where?...

The four friends stood silently. King broke the silence.
"Hang on a minute, he whispered. Hang on, I can feel something?".
Eight pairs of ears immediately pricked up!.
"Can you feel that?",queried King..
The others stared at each other..."Feel what?", replied Meowla?

Then suddenly they all felt it.

It was a low, a very low rumbling.

The rumble grew! Until it became a shake, and a rumble.

Then the shaking and rumbling became as one!

Louder and louder was the shaking and rumbling, until it became one thunderous cacophony of sound and vibration.

That was when the light appeared.

From the ruins of the slain tree shot beams, and bolts of green light.

The light grew in intensity, and brightness, until the whole area of woodland was bursting, with warm and green pulsating light!

At the same time on Two legger World the same thing was happening.

Jack and Sheila, Mum and Dad and Mr. Moneygrabber were all in the den. Mr. Moneygrabber had been looking at Benson.

"I'm sorry, he had said, but Benson has died. He must have sli[pped away in his sleep!".

He was just in the process of explaining, to the grief stricken family, that they wern't to worry. He would deal with everything. For a small fee, of course.

As this was going on, they had suddenly been struck to silence, as the lights appeared!

Jack noticed it first!

"Look at the windows", he exclaimed.

They had all turned to see. The whole sky outside the window, had become a bright green glow!

Sheila and Jack ran over to the window and looked down at their garden.

Sure enough, the area in the garden, that had been home to the stricken Yew Tree, was now ablaze with the strange green light show. Beams were pouring out of the earth, and lighting the sky, from where the ruins of the tree once stood.

At the same time they could see, dawn was breaking.
For the first time in the three days since the great storms
had started, dawn was putting in an appearence.
Suddenly, a great mist decended on everything outside
ther window.
The mist kind of seemed to drop from, the sky itself.
Leaving it bright, blue and clear, whilst covering the
earth like a huge duvet.
All of a sudden, as they watched in fact, the mist just
sort of evaporated in on itself.
It just cleared away, as if it had never been there in the
first place.
It left a cool, bright, and most beautiful, Spring style
morning in it's wake.
"Look,said Jack, quietly to his sister.."Look".
Sheila gasped at what met her gaze..
There, in the corner of the front garden, where the Yew
Tree had stood. There, amongst the ruined wood, and
foliage, was a tall green shoot.
It was a tall green shoot. But it was also the beginnings
of a strong young tree.
A Yew Tree...

The ground tremors and thunderous rumblings, were at
their highest pitch yet. The light was so bright, that our
four animal friends had to hide their eyes.
Until it just STOPPED!!
All was silent...
King, Bounce,Meowla and Old Joe slowly uncovered
their eyes.
The brightness had eased and their vision was clearing.
They soon heard heard a familiar rustle.
Then, out of the ground appeared a bough, and then a
branch.
They seemed to shoot directly upwards, towards, the
now blue tinted sky.
More followed, then more followed that.

At the same time, these boughs, and branches started to merge into one great trunk. A great tree trunk.
Suddenly, the light exploded into bright green brilliance.
Then all was quiet. As quickly as it had appeared, the light faded.
Leaving our four friends, standing in the wooded copse.
They raised their eyes and looked at where thelights had been.
There he was!.
A smile on his big craggy face.
There stood The Mighty Protector.
The Happiness Tree lived.
Oh Great Tree, you live!". said King, as he bowed low, in homage to the great tree.
"Yes!!".. boomed The Happiness Tree.
Thanks to you all..I live. The worlds live!
Ragnar is no more..The Black Wolf sleeps - the eternal sleep.
"But Benson is dead!", Bounce woofed sadly.
Oh Great Tree, Benson could not return with us?".
Benson's sacrifice was indeed, a terrible one, my children".
"But dead?".
"I think not!!
"Turn around my four children!, turn around and behold your saviour!!"..
The four friends slowly turned around..
Meowla purred like she had never had occasion to purr before, King howled and woofed. Bounce yapped, and jumped around, like little dogs do!
Old Joe started singing and sqeaking and attempted to woof!!
There, sitting proudly on his haunches, was a very young looking Benson The Dog.
He grinned his Staffie grin at his friends, and jumped to his feet.

There was lots of kissing, licking, sniffing and tail chasing going on, in the now green and sunny Sleepy Dog Land.

The Happiness Tree watched his children play.

So proud of them was the Great Wooded Protector.

So very proud of his dear children.

"But wait!!", boomed The Happiness Tree.

"Let's have some quiet...!"

"I would speak..!!".

The five friends sat in front of the Great Tree and listened.

The tree continued.

"I am proud of you all. Proud, and much humbled by the courage, and bravery you ALL have shown".

"Sleepy Dog Land is once again safe. This time it will be eternal safety.

Evil has been vanquished by one unselfish act".

"The ancient words have been used. The ancient magic holds us all together, in it's mystical arms".

"You all are safe. Benson, you gave the supreme sacrifice. No thought for yourself. Your soul was indeed taken in Ragnar's Dark and Fabled Lands.

"But, because of your unselfish act, death could not hold you".

"Your spirit now free, to fly back into your stricken body!!".

"Because of what has happened, all in Sleepy Dog Land, and the many other lands that surround it. All will live".

"On Two legger earth. Now all will live. My children the trees, re-grow as we speak".

"Harmony has returned to our lands, harmony for all things, and all creatures.

The debt is paid - and the magic now appeased"!!.

We will all live, and we will learn. There will be many more adventures to come, here in Sleepy Dog Land.

"But tradgedy has been averted! No more will evil ever enter, or stalk these Sleepy Lands".

"But Benson, I think it is time for you to go?
Benson put his big head on one side ...."Time to go sir?..he queried.
"Yes, Benson. There are two small two leggers, who are very sad.!".
"Their help was also invaluble!!".
"Now go to them!".
Benson nodded and wagged his tail big style..He was so excitied.
He said farewell to his friends, promising to see them later.
With that, he padded over to The Happiness Tree, and lay down.
Benson closed his eyes, and in the shade of The Mighty Protector.
Benson slept.

After the amazing happenings in the garden, all was now rather quiet and sombre in Two Legger world.
Mr. Moneygrabber, the vet, was talking with Dad.
Mum sat sadly, looking out of the Den window.
Jack and Sheila, were sitting in great misery, next to Benson, on the sofa.
Suddenly Jack jumped up!
"Wah!",he spluttered.
"What is it Jack asked Sheila..What's the matter?".
"It's Benson, shouted Jack..He moved?".
The room went quiet.
Mum, Dad, Mr. Moneygrabber and the two children, stood looking at the dog on the sofa.
"Look!!, screamed Sheila, H-he's moving..
Sure enough, as they watched, they saw Benson's chest rise and fall.
It was as if he had been swimming underwater, and had to rush to the surface for air.
He made a sharpe intake of breath!.
It was all smiles in the den.
Benson, lifted his head, and looked around.

Sheila and Jack rushed to him, they cuddled him and stroked him and generally fussed and fussed!

Benson The Dog loved it!!

The only person in the room who seemed, a bit out of sorts, was Mr. Moneygrabber. Dad said later, it was because now the vet would not get any further fees for treatment of Benson.

They all laughed at this.

Also it is worth mentioning that the whole world was in celebration at the sudden change in the weather.

The news reports came thick and fast.

In the Forest Of Dean, for example, where ever a tree had died, or fallen, small young trees now grew in their place.

This was happening the world over.

All was re-birth.

Benson was back home and safe.

He lay in the lounge licking his paws.

Also he felt so much better now.

No aches and pains in his joints. No weakness or sickness.

In fact, he felt a great deal younger, than he had, before all these adventures had begun.

Benson lay in the lounge.

"Hmm, thought Benson,I'm bored? I'm bored, bored bored.

He smiled to himself.

"I may be bored, he thought, but I am more than happy, to be bored, as bored can be.

Benson The Dog was not complaining..

He lay his head on his paws, and drifted into sleep.

You can all guess where he is off to?

Because as the poetry says...

When our dogs take a nap so their spirits take flight
straight to Sleepy Dog Land
anytime - day or night.
Safe in Sleepy Dog Land

where all dogs may roam free
or hangout with their mates
"neath The Happiness Tree.
Tasty treats there aplenty
lushous grass just to chew
anything they could want for
every wish will come true.
Such a magical haven
where no dog has a care
It's a realm of true wonder
In amidst of a prayer.

The End.

Join us again soon!
For many more Tales From Sleepy Dog Land.
Next in the series:
Tales From Sleepy Dog Land Book 3.
"Undercover Strays.
I would just like to dedicate this book to my darling
wife Sheila, and to my dear son Ashley.
Their help, love and support has been constant - and
unconditional.
Of course a huge THANKYOU to our resident hero:
Benson The Dog.

Lightning Source UK Ltd.
Milton Keynes UK
UKOW05f1129091014

239801UK00010B/168/P